EVEN THE RED HERON

Julian Feeld

This paperback edition published in 2014
by FEELD Publishing

Copyright © Julian Peverelli, 2014

The moral right of the author has been asserted

ISBN-13: 978-1495414695
ISBN-10: 1495414698

Extract of "The Princess and the Pea"
by Hans Christian Andersen, 1835 (Public Domain)

Extract of "Caja de Sorpresas"
© El Gran Combo de Puerto Rico, 1982

Author's note:

The following text is comprised of two parts.

Part I includes transcribed entries from Daniel and Sarah's respective diaries. All grammatical inaccuracies and spelling mistakes have been reproduced exactly as they exist in their source texts. The other chapters are written records of Abilena's inner monologues.

Part II is a chronological set of transcriptions culled from the minds of several different characters.

to sister, mother, her sister, and their mother

"This Crisis Has Caught Us Without Strategy"

–Headline, EL NACIONAL
21st of February, 1983

I

Daniel — 19 of April of 1997

Billys in the mountainside and so will I be. Conio I hope its quiet then. But what if hes waiting for me under the grass? Im not gonna kill myself and find out. Instead Im gonna write every thing down so his voice stops running circles and circles in my head. I tried writing spanish but it felt bad because spanish is for talking shit with the others in the bar and theres no others and no bar out here. Its lonely country up here in the mountains. Conio viejo stop it with the pity. Nobody gives a fuck about you. Your brains like an old yamaha 55 outboard with no filter so the gas is full of water and the fucking thing wont start. No way to clean the carb neither. What a mess. Theres too many thoughts coming at the same time and too many thoughts about how things started. How things were at the beginning when I had hope and loved Sarah and wasnt a fucking huevon living in a shack with nothing exept a dog. I call him fucker when he reminds me of me. Even hunting and gardning doesnt make the thoughts stop. Maybe someone will find this journal and make me famous. The kind of famous where people remember you because you screwd everything up so much it became ART. See your just like Abilena viejo no difference. HA HA HA. Theres nothing pretty about you. Your only good at making money and your not even good at that. Thats all I cared about. And thats what Sarah cared about too. MONEY MONEY MONEY the poisonous fucking money. After Abilena was born I took a loan from the bank and bought the house in Boca De Uchire. Sarah complained we couldnt aford it but I knew what she meant. I couldnt aford her. I had become a Venezolano but she was still an expat always hanging around with gringos. Being an expat meant owning a beach house so I bought her one 2 hours outside Caracas if you drive fast. It was stuck between the open ocean and a shallow laguna filled with flamingos. They built the compound on concrete so it wouldnt sink into the muddy sandbar. Really OKAY construction all and all. Our neighbors were all foreners and polite. Even a French family came there sometimes with their kids who cried when they played with Abilena. Abilena was a tough kid. She didnt play mean but she didnt behave like a lady neither. The house was just east along the coast after Tacarigua National Park. It was a beach house where we could come relax when we had free time. But I never had free time. I was too busy working for the GODDAMN MONEY so my family could SPEND IT. I remember busines was good and we were supposed to live a life of leesure and be part the new middle class. It was important to Sarah. She pretended it wasnt but I knew it was. Back then everything seemed possible too. New gringos had arived with expensive fishing gear and they were willing to pay crazy money to fish the peacock bass. Suddenly the CASH was FLOWING again. It made me real happy to own a lake even though it was small and very far inland. That was the bad part. A good ride from both the beach house and Caracas and I was still paying back the loan. Good thing the gringos were coming because fishing was slow there for awile. Javier and Carlos couldnt believe their goddamn eyes when they saw californians pulling hundreds from their pockets. Every day theyd take these sunburned idiots out in the rusty old dingys to fish and smoke cubans and drink ice cold POLAR. But the boys could tell I was a nigger to the new gringos. They kept calling me jefe but only because they felt sorry for me. Anyways I could never convince them to call me danny. Even though Ive lived here most of my life Im still a gringo to them and that means I run things and they dont. But I havent been to Arkansas since I was a real youngun like 11 or 12. I cant remember. Dont want to neither. Fuck America. I have no dreams of apple pie or American tits or sundaes or the dumb farmers at school or my roten fucking dad or the stupid farm neither. Abilena and Billy were born here like real Venezuelans even though he had his mothers pale skin that boy and Bibi was fragile when she was a little baby skwirming in her crib with those blue eyes making my haert melt. Back when Bibi was born Sarah and I still got along real good. We were young and dumb and I took out a loan so the bank gave it to me straight. They told me SIR THIS IS A RISKY LOAN. They told me If I defolted on my payments I standed a chance to lose everything. The lake and the house. Both houses. But I went for it anyway because the crisp dollars were washing up on the shores. It was the dream of the mid 60s really. Thousands of idiots with visor caps and fany packs and plenty of peacock bass to go around. I owned a real entrepise an honest to god fishing business with a LOGO and a NAME and a REPUTATION. Even Sarah was happy. So I uped the prices and the customers kept rolling in. Things were different back then. Kennedy was done with his fucking head blown all over the hood of the limo. Im not sure Kennedy woulda done it better anyway. Politicians are SCUM. Kennedys brains going splat and his wife clawing around like a panick chicken. Then Betancourt was smart enough to step down before they did the same to him. When he resined he tried to make it sound OK but I could tell he was scared shitless. He left behind the type of democracy the gringos really love. Venezuela would be electing her leaders but nobody was gona fuck with Chevron or Texaco. Leoni got elected by promising jobs to the pueblo and Venezuela started looking like a real international player. The oil was gona make us all rich wether the communists liked it or not. Wed bring in those dumb gringos and get them all fishing. They loved me because I was a good old boy. Id speak their language so theyd get comfortable and loosen their wallets. Who cares if they thought I was a hick. I owned a beach house and a fancy British wife. Sarah was the type of woman youd find a perl in her clam. Respectable. This was at the beginning when Abilena was born. Before it all went to shit.

For the Dogs (Age 6)

I know daddy's keeping the dogs away from his meat, cause even from the shower I can hear the coins rattle in the old coffee can he uses to hurt their ears. Mom said dinner. Hope he cooks it long so there's no blood.

Turn the rusty knob on the cement shower and the sand's more sticky when the water's not splashing it. Then there's the walk on the broken black stepping stones so I don't put my toes in the sand, but there's always sand on the damn rocks anyway, so I ain't happy bout it. There's old burnt pieces of wood too, hiding in the sand, but they won't burn again unless they've been burning from before.

Also don't want a shard from the palm leaves in my toes, then the sand'll get into my blood and it'll stay there forever. Some people died forever from having things inside they couldn't get out, like the red rust on the side of the coffee can or the big nails from the broken fishing boats.

When the waves push the fishing boats to the rocks they split em right open and the men have to swim in the dark with fish hung round their necks.

Still I walk over the stones on my tippy-toes to reach the dirt path between the little houses. They're orange in the evening light and the wind's blowing through the palms so I look up and

Coconuts! They'll crack your head if you ain't careful. Then it's time for the hospital where they put stitches through your hair until you're bleeding from the string. So I keep an eye on the coconuts when they're in the wind.

Even wrapped in the towel it's damn cold and I look back at the fat wooden gate sitting in the darkness between the grey showers. It's not moving. You should always close the wooden gate so thieves don't come into the compound from the beach and take Daddy's grill and Bill's surfboard like two summers ago when the thieves came. They're trained out there with knives and they'll come quick and quiet behind you.

If there's one thing I hate it's sand in my toes and thieves coming through the gate. When I grow up I won't be scared of nothing, not even them, cause then I'll be a mommy and have a big strong man to hold me tight. There's one for each woman, mom told me. Try sneaking then, cause you won't be able to, swear it on mom's head.

Dinner, mom's yelping, dinner and it's getting cold. I'm shivering and have goose pimples all over my elbows and knees. The worst's the mosquito bites I'll tell you. The water infects them with all the salty garbage. It's true, I've seen plastic bags and watches and rotten jellyfish carried by the tides and left on the beach without her babies to die.

But the shower took care of that so when I rub my towel I'm just careful with the mosquito bites. That's where the *dengue* fevers come from. The mosquito bites.

We got the screen door closed and I check to make sure dogs ain't thieving through my legs to get inside the house.

There you are. I was wondering what you were doing out there. You're gonna drive your poor old mother crazy. What have I told you about staying out after dark?

I was just showering but I closed the gate, mom.

Hm. Put on a dress and join us for dinner. Your father cooked *bife con patatas fritas*.

Well the fan ain't turning in my room, so I put my undies and dress on. No bra why? Not til I'm a big girl.

Sit down at the table. Dad smells sweet and my hair's sticky but mom don't care cause we're in vacation. Meat smells good but we say grace by holding hands and mommy says grace.

Thank you lord for the food on this table and for our health. Thank you for bringing William back to this family and keeping us safe from harm. Amen.

Bill's sitting cross from me and says nothing. His hands ain't together for grace. He's just looking at the *bife* and his mouth doesn't move an inch. Eyeballs red like a fish's gut.

I eat the green beans first and save the best for last. Dip the fries in ketchup but they're not good, they have the skin on em like mom always does. She says it's the best part, but I know they're not good.

Stop playing with your food, young lady.

Sorry, mom.

Food is for eating, but she's smiling and I finish all the fries.

Now eat your *bife*, young lady. It's getting cold.

When I push the knife in, the juice starts coming out and it's pink and mixes with the old ketchup. Blood from the cow's in my *bife* so I take the piece and put it on my knee. There's blood running down my leg and onto my foot and toes. The floor's squishy. I cut more pieces and push em onto my knee when mom's not looking.

Bill's looking at me. He knows there's blood all over my knee and down my leg and on the floor.

I'll clean it up, Bill, but I don't tell him or they'll hear. I'll clean it up. But he doesn't tattle.

When my plate's empty it's a little swimming pool of blood and ketchup and I ask to be excused from the table. Daddy's sweetness is strong from the rum and his breathing's like a running dog or a horse with big black nose holes.

You don't want dessert?

No thank you.

But I baked plantain, Abi. It's delicious. You love *platanos* with cinnamon.

No thank you.

I pull the meat into my hands and there's too much blood on my knee. I wipe it with my elbows but they can't see.

Do you need to go to the bathroom, young lady?

No.

Then why are you squirming like that?

For nothing.

You can go to the bathroom.

Thanks.

I stand up but my hands aren't big enough and a piece of *bife* falls between my legs and splats on the floor. Mommy's eyes are big and round with a mouth, but Bill doesn't move at all. Dad stands slowly, breathing down on me. He's very tall.

I work hard for the money I bring home to this family.

Danny

You shut up. I'm talking to her. Money doesn't grow on trees. Do you realize that?

Yes, Daddy, but there was cow's blood in my *bife* and I don't like blood.

Do you know what you are? A spoiled brat.

But I don't wanna eat blood.

Don't answer back to your father.

In the war they would execute a man for not eating his food. And look at you throwing it away when there's starving kids in Africa.

Then send it to them so they can eat it!

So the stinging is like mustard in my nose and there's red pain tingling in my cheeks. It's not fair how I'm crying. It was too late when I tried not to start. Now there's wet everywhere and Bill's sitting with red eyes while mom wrestles Daddy and holds her wrists.

You do not hit my daughter! You do not hit my daughter! I will divorce you!

The door slams behind me and I throw meat to the dogs who chew and fight and bark. I'm crying in my mouth and it's salty. The dogs lick their rotten teeth and disgusting pink mouths. They're breathing around me and licking my knees and legs and tickling my toes. I'm crying and laughing and slapping their heads and their tongues lick my wet kneecaps and skinny legs.

The windows make big yellow squares of light on the outside. Other than that, the night's dark and wet as the voices quiet down. A big moon up, and stars too, and I lie on my back on the cold concrete as the stars become a blanket, real close to my face so I can reach out easily and feel its soft surface. Don't even care about the sand in my hair, although it's probably rubbing very nasty. Just mom sobbing, a real pretty sound actually, and soon the door whines open and Daddy walks out, the small red dot of his cigarette floating in the darkness. Smoke is dark blue and Daddy's shining round with light from the windows, like the paintings of jesus, cept jesus never smoked. I don't move much and he doesn't say nothing and his steps are real close to my head as he walks by without touching me. I stay quiet and my eyes are used to the dark now. I can see the red brick walls, low and separating the little homes, and even the palm trees standing up to the moon. Mom's crying and Bill says nothing as the car coughs onto the main road. After a long time with just me and the blanket, the dogs sniffing but not licking, the mosquitoes biting plenty, and the car somewhere else, mom comes to the door and stands looking out. She can't see me cause mom's not used to the night and her eyes ain't good for much.

Abilena! Abi!

Mom's face is very tired. There's lots of makeup dribbled from her eyeballs and dark moons underneath em.

Abilena. Are you out there? Abi.

Then she goes inside. Soon the window to her bedroom goes dark. After some more quiet and one of the dogs licking my nose, Bill's skinny face pops at the window and he sees me quick.

Pequeña.

Bill.

Let's go crabbing.

Ok.

Bill pulls me up. My head and my butt hurt plenty from the hard cement. We walk with no sound to the gate and out through the sidehole with lots of sand in my undies already. Bill's skinny but strong, and he pulls me up again.

On the beach the boats're upside down and the paint's chipped and watered with shining. Even the sand's pretty wet, all bunched and hard under the feet. Bill clicks the flashlight and it shoots a black circle inside a yellow circle, just like the moon when it covers the sun. Then it moves over the sand like a detective because Bill tells me to follow him. There's tiny holes in the sand with little squiggles of dirt where the worms pushed in, but I ain't never seen none. The crab holes are bigger, and you can usually see half a crab, or the whole crab sometimes. Many of them don't even have a hole and they're just running sideways on the sand, zigzagging with their little white clippers.

Here. Hold it.

I wave the yellow circle round. Not too far from Bill, cause it's dark. He fiddles for a while and then lights a big cigarette, sorta like Dad's but different. Then he lets me keep the flashlight and we walk right up to the water where it's foaming little bubbles.

Sometimes the foam's dry and hard, and then it goes away when you touch it like cotton candy. There's the sea grass in clumps, rotten fishnets, and chewed up orange floaters. Those are real bright under the flashlight. Then I spot a crab, a real white one with a big brain under his shell. I run after him, but he's too fast and escapes home to his wife.

Do you want some of this?

What is it, Bill?

It'll make you feel funny.

Funny how?

Funny like cartoons on the tv, with colors and stuff.

How do I do it?

He passes me the cigarette and shows me how to suck and get the smoke out. Then you have to hold your breath like you're underwater and cough like Dad's car and you're crabbing with Bill under the stars. The moon's moving fast on the sand and I chase it with the crabs. I have to dance sideways to make sure everything works. Bill's laughing and I'm dancing like a crab and he gives me first prize. He makes the moon and I chase it. After a while I'm very sticky and we find a log. Bill hits the log with his toe and says dirt. I take off my dress and undies and fold them real neat on the log, above the crabs and the moon and the sand, and we run into the ocean together, falling into the crashing waves, dark and warm and lovely. The moon's back in the sky and Bill chops it with his claws. I can see his naked butt and the chopped moon floating in pieces over the waves. When Bill kicks the water it makes floating stars and we swim through them. Then he stops moving and I wait for the stars to come back, but they don't because they're gone.

Don't let them kill you, *pequeña*.

But the stars won't hurt me.

You gotta stay alive despite mom and dad. Promise me.

I look at Bill and his eyes're wet.

Are you ok, Bill?

I hug his skinny arms.

Fuck, *pequeña*. Don't listen to me.

We lie on our backs in the sand. My head's on Bill's arm and there's shivering but I feel warm. The blanket's everywhere actually, and there's stars in everything. I'm gonna remember this forever til my eyes are old and I can't see nothing. Promise. I'll live with Bill, king of the crabs, moon cutter, brother Bill and his lovely stars.

Sarah — March 4th, 1996

Today we ate fried *mandioca*, rice, beans, and mashed apples for the sixth day in a row. I'm sick of it. I asked Anna-Felicia if we could switch roles, but she refused, the ill-tempered cow. I'm pretty sure she doesn't use any salt or pepper. I think she puts cinnamon in the *mandioca* and sugar in the beans. That woman does not deserve to cook for us. I don't care how many years she spent cleaning the toilet block, I still think it remains a more fitting role for her. The other sisters have been living out here in isolation for so many years that they can no longer discern good from bad. It's the only explanation I have for their placid indifference. They treat me like a child if I ever have the gall to complain, which makes me furious to no end. A-F has been watching me like a hawk to ensure I finish my food. She must have noticed me scraping my dish into the compost bin. In today's Giving Of Thanks she included "never wasting our God-given food". Can you believe it? She's out to get me. I know it. I miss meat and cake. I even miss Coca Cola. Pathetic, I know.

Claudia was very helpful in today's tutoring session. She has such a wonderfully precise vocabulary, all things considered! It must be her German lineage. What's nice about Claudia is that she's not rigid like most of the other Germans I've known. She's very kind and gentle, but doesn't hesitate to "tell it as it is" (to use a rather unfortunate American term). She speaks very slowly and deliberately, and I've taken to recording many of the things she says. Later I underline the best parts so that I can make progress. Today's jewel: "Because we have vowed to break from our old lives and join a higher order, we must recall with full clarity the faulty relationships of our past and the defects of character which inadvertently caused these missteps. Do not worry if your mind meanders, but when you notice the inevitable drift, simply catch gentle hold of the rudder and firmly steer the ship back on course." I've corrected a few grammatical mistakes, of course, as Claudia's English isn't always of the highest quality. Her vocabulary is spectacular, but her sentences have a tendency to be quite sparse.

Recently she asked me to write about Daniel when I "felt ready to". That's probably why I've been blowing the gaff. I would much rather write about cinnamon and beans than examine my marriage to Daniel. It's taken isolation and prayer to fully conjure his ghost. I picture him not in his later state of dereliction but instead as his younger self, wild-eyed and full of explosive vigour, at an age when he was still a force to be reckoned with. Say what you will about Daniel, the man certainly knew how to make an entrance.

He might catch the men's attention first. They would turn to him like nervous pups sensing a predator, especially the "leaders" among them. He never paid them any mind. Instead he would make the rounds, slapping each boy on the back as if they were old fellows at a reunion, and nodding absent-mindedly to the girls or even kissing them on the hand if he were especially fond of them. I'm sure he was the topic of many bedroom conversations. I seem to remember there having been an attempt to have "the yank" (as they called him) permanently evicted from our parties, on the pretext that he was neither a student nor a member of faculty. The girls adored him though, and a few of the boys found him harmless or even amusing, so eventually the whole effort fell apart. After Daniel caught wind of the failed scheme, he would often stand on a table, beer in hand, rambling wildly about the nobility of the student body, the importance of higher education, the physical prowess of the modern British male, etcetera.

At first he seemed to take no notice of my presence at these get-togethers (if only I had understood men's tricks like I do now!) I can even remember him claiming to be a shy man (although his demeanor radiated absolute confidence). And so this period of distance did not last, (oh how I wish now that he had found some other distraction!) and he soon went out of his way to sidle up to me at parties, pin me beneath those blue eyes of his, and press me with the type of relentless questions only a child would ask a parent. That's what he was, looking back. Just a child in need of a mother. Of course I was young and oblivious at the time, and found his curious drawl quite charming. His energy dissolved the stale academic atmosphere and awoke in me an appetite for hazard. What's more he owned a car and traveled with ease between the expat circles and "real Venezuela" (as he often called it). Yes, Daniel was everything I found myself wanting. A real cowboy ready to take me on the wild South American adventure.

Daddy's War (Age 6)

There's plenty sticky everywhere at the beach. Daddy's little radio got sticky inside and stopped working completely.

Who touched it?

Nobody touched it, honey, nobody ever touches your radio.

Always listening to the news in quick yelling, shut up and let Daddy listen to the goddamn news. Words like black spit from the grey box, hot in the sun with a cigarette listening to the goddamn news. After it don't work, even though it wasn't me, I figured stay away. Daddy gets angry when things don't work and he screamed and screamed until I stopped hiding because he broke into it like a thief. Daddy's a delicate thief, with strong delicate fingers, a proud fingers if I say so myself. When he opened it up, there was a red sickness inside. Everything was covered in red dust, a wet dust like leaves in water pipes when they go bad.

Like Bill's hair when it shines in the sun and he smiles with his eyebrows up cause he's happy. Bill's got stars all over his skin too, and they protect him from the sun, but he's gotta use special sunscreen to help his powers work. One day he explained it all to me, one day he'll explain it all. He's safe from the sun and doesn't much like it, truth's in the pudding. He'll sit plenty times under the palm roof and read books in the hammock. Just sitting in the dark with a book by Stephen King.

I don't like scary books. Bill told me about a girl with pig's blood on her head and I didn't want to hear it, but he held me down under his knees and told me about her bloody hair and laughed red and brown and black.

But everything's sticky and sandy at the beach. The sofa pillows are covered in chipped plastic, sometimes hard with little brown pimples. Dad makes them with his cigarette as he falls asleep. They're little holes. I always keep a towel on top of them to make sure nothing nasty gets inside me. I could catch a red sickness like Daddy's radio and stop working completely. No way. That's not the plan, Stan.

When something doesn't move, there's no noise. When something moves, there's always plenty noise. Like Daddy's coffee can when he uses it to scare the dogs, or the big wooden fan hanging over my bed when it turns in circles. Even the dogs make noises when they scuffle in the bushes or scratch the cement. Their tongues run up and down when they make breathing noises after they run. See?

Every time I get in bed I make sure to scrape all the sands off my feet so they don't get in bed with me, but there's always sands in the sheets no matter what. When I wake up there's plenty and I can see the sun coming through the window to make the room hotter again. I'm plenty sticky already, with that morning stick. Even the sands get sticky and won't leave. I'm gonna be a sand monster one day, cross my heart and hope to die. But even though the pillows of the grey couches are sticky, the only best pillow is the one from my bed, the one I bring from Caracas. It makes cold underneath it, and when it's real hot, I just flip it over and steal it all with my face. Then I forget about the sand and the mosquitoes and the little brown pimples. Til it's hot again.

If I was a mosquito I wouldn't try to fly through the netting cause the holes are too small. I'd just find a bigger hole like the brown pimples or make one with a cigarette. Daddy would be a good mosquito, even though he bites harder than most. It always stings a lot but there's never any itch. That's the worst part about the bites, really. I'm itching right now, all up and down my legs on the red bumps. Can't help it none, even though mom always says you shouldn't, it only makes things worst and worst.

There's another kind of itch. Sometimes a mosquito bites between my legs, where I have a hole to pee from, and my pillow helps me take care of it. I tried it on the other bites but it doesn't work. If you use the pillow to rub the hole, it gets better and better until you're better than you started before the bite. It can work a few times too. Depends which mosquito bites you. Then your eyes are droopy and your feets and hands feel like pepsi cola. Even with sand it's ok to fall asleep sometimes, and you bet your bottom I'll keep this pillow til forever and ever. Only trouble is you pee a little, but only a little and then it dries.

Mom never finds out like she used to. I used to pee

a swimming pool and the mattress would get painted yellow. Then we'd have to dry it again on the side of the house, with the neighbors all talking about Abilena, that yellow stainer Abi, she done it again. It's written in yellow all over the house, really. That yellow stainer. But Bill never says nothing about it and Daddy doesn't even know. Mom puts all the mattresses out there and just tells em it's cleaning time. Bill knows though. He always knows everything but never tells anyone about it. Bill's probably surfing right now, but they took his board. He's surfing cept for that.

I'm more or less hungry even though I could scratch some more at these bites. There's plenty sun to enjoy.

I get up and my undies are twisted sideways so I pull them right and walk out into the kitchen. My butt scratches and the smell of my finger's sweet, feet cold on the tile as I reach for the rice crispies. Pour plenty into a bowl but not enough to spill. Then I add sugar and white milk, cold white milk.

Through the mosquito netting I can see the strong sun and Daddy's hair shining like a spoon, with the sunglasses and all the blonde handsome. Daddy's smoking and looking down the path to the gate, with no shirt and his blonde hair shining.

I leave the bowl in the sink for mom and creep out through the swinging door like a thief. The cement's warm as warm can get, and I know Daddy won't be too sweet cause he's drinking beer. Beer's not too sweet, believe me, I tasted it once when he was sleeping and it wasn't nothing sweet. I'm coming up the path crawling until Daddy's shoulders block the light. They're big and brown and smooth. Then I crawl through his legs and he closes them like a gate. I'm trapped!

Bibi, you little monkey. What do you think you're doing? I'll show you what happens to sneaky little monkeys. They get tickled.

I try to run but it's too late and Daddy's tickling my belly until I taste some milk. He's kissing my cheek and saying

Bibi, Bibi, my little monkey princess Bibi. I'm your gorilla king and don't you ever forget it.

He's a little sweet but I don't mind none. He holds me high and I can see all the little houses from the mountain on Daddy's shoulders, like a pirate with a telescope looking at all the sunny islands.

There's other families but we're the best one. When we run down the path I can feel all the bounces til we get to the palm roof and dad lifts me onto it.

Uh-oh. You might have to live up there for a few days, until I come back to save you.

I'm climbing all the palm leaves cause they're dry and piled into a roof. At the top there's a perfect wooden hat to hold onto. I can see the surfers in the waves rolling up and down, sitting on their boards or tumbling in the splash. The little huts like mushrooms with people under them. Some of them broken or empty. All the pieces of wood look like fish guts, bent in a twirl and horning out of the sand.

Some of the plants are good and some of the plants are bad. Bad are the little plants with nothing to do, just little thorns and plenty dirt. Good are the big smooth plants with their shiny smiling leaves like the belly of a green slimeless fish. Never break a good plant, it'll go sticky and get ruined.

Abi, come down now before you get killed.

I can hear Daddy's voice underneath the umbrella, like he's out in the ocean yelping in. I'm walking carefully down the front of the cone but it doesn't the matter, the roof still cracks dry under both feet and I yelp for help as I fall!

Both fingers holding, my feet dangling

Daddy yelping

Let go, let go!

I'm not gonna, I'm not gonna. But my fingers hurt so I slip and fall and hit the cement, but it's soft as a cloud. Only my neck hurts a bit.

I got you. I got you Bibi. Don't worry. Don't you worry.

But I'm not crying, cause I don't cry anymore. I'm not a stupid little baby falling to die from her crib.

Are you ok? Are you alright?

Daddy's eyes are bright blue and shining big, and there's nothing sweet about em. They're like glass when it's fancy. I can see right into Daddy and he's got some water on his lashes. He's like a boat inside a bottle.

Everything's fine.

There's a long time happens before Daddy puts me down to walk. We get to the beach then, through the gate and onto the burning sand. I have to run ahead of him, from island to island where the darker sand sleeps in the shadows. Daddy doesn't run.

Once we get to the water line I'm looking everywhere. Maybe I'll find a watch, or a bottle with a secret message inside, or a pair of new shoes the water ain't even touched. Or some bills. If a ship full of money exploded, there would be money bills floating to the beach. We'd find them all day! But there's only a jellyfish. Jellyfishes don't breathe cause they're made of dangerous chewing gum. Daddy stands over me until there's shade on the jellyfish. There's sand in his hole and his little folds too.

Is he dead?

Damn thing never lived in the first place.

Daddy's smoke gives me coughing and I lean closer to the jellyfish. There's pretty little fingers made of dark blue jello. Then the jellyfish is made of light blue hoolyhoops and a milky white ball in the middle. There's still some blue inside the ball though, and it's making melt.

One of our neighbors has jellyfishes in his eyes. He can't see none. He's full of milk and walks around with a stick, tapping shapes to get places. Mom says he's like a dolphin sending out messages with his stick cause his eyes don't work. Sometimes that happens when you get too old. I don't touch the jellyfish cause I don't wanna pee. Maybe he's making the sand around him bad. He's got too much sand in him. That's the jellyfish problem.

I look up at Daddy smiling with his big white teeth. The middle ones are yellow from kissing cigarettes all the time. Daddy's pushing the wet sand into the dry sand, so I take big lumps of it and make a mountain. Then Daddy makes a hole in the mountain and we have a bridge. Under the bridge is a hole with water at the bottom. It never gets dry, no matter how much you dig. We try to protect the bridge with a wall, but the water keeps making it muddy. So Dad builds the wall until it reaches his knees, but still it doesn't work.

Daddy.

Yes Bibi.

What happened to your finger?

You know what happened to my finger, Bibi. I've told you a thousand times.

Yes Daddy, but I like it when you tell me. It's not the same when I just think about it.

I lost my finger in the Korean war.

The war with fish?

Well sometimes fish died in the war, but mostly it was humans. Good men.

And you hit people in the war?

Only from very far. I was a sniper. I would hide in the mountains and surprise people.

You used a gun on them?

A rifle. With a telescope on it. I could see everything from far.

And did the people die?

Some of them.

Your rifle killed them.

Yes, sometimes.

How many people did your rifle kill?

Hundreds.

I show Daddy all my fingers.

How many times?

Ten times all of those.

And then you stopped?

Then I stopped.

Where was I?

You weren't born yet. It was just your mother and me. She waited the whole war. It was very brave of her.

I push the sand for a bit. The sun is falling and Daddy has a new can of beer in his pocket. I use the old one to build a tower. It's strong from the metal. Even water can't hurt my tower now.

So the fish took your finger?

No fish. Something bad happened to my rifle. Part of it blew up. They couldn't find my finger.

It disappeared?

Yes.

And then the *piraña* fish ate it.

No goddamn fish, Bibi. I already fucking told you. Do I have to tell you three times?

No, Daddy.

When Daddy tells me things three times, there's always noise. All Daddies get really angry about saying things three times. So it's better to shut up. Still I know the *piraña* fish made his finger special, cause Daddy told me when he was sweet.

I bet there's fish living in the hole under the bridge. Be careful or they'll swim up inside you. That's why I don't sit in the hole, cause it's for babies and tadpoles. And the ocean is full of fish too. I can feel them with my eyes, snaking through the seaweed to bite me. And I know about the *piraña* fish too, the way he sneaks through the grass and eats a whole cow in three blinks. Then he eats you. Maybe the ocean would be safer if Daddy made a wall of cows out in the water. Then if one of them disappeared we could yelp and save everybody by running. See you later, alligator. Cows are just *bife* and they don't hurt much anyway. They even like it when we eat em.

The sand around the can's falling again and again. Keep sticking it back, but it won't stay up. Daddy's sitting on a log and smoking a cigarette, looking at the droopy sky. It's sunny but also plenty droopy when Daddy doesn't say nothing, just like Billy and the jellyfish. I got sand in my bikini and it's rubbing and itching. My butt's sandy and the wall's falling from what Daddy built. I look at the stupid hole full of wet sand. So Dad's like Bill except his arms are bigger and browner, he has a special finger, and he doesn't never read.

Daniel — 24 of April of 1997

OLD DANNY FUCKUP. Old danny fuckup gonna die up here alone. Old danny fuckups what they call me yeah. Im like Bob Dylan when I write poetry. HA HA HA. Nobodys laughing though. I used to wait for so many things. If I could get all my ducks in a row things would be great and Id be happy. Now theres nothing waiting for me but a hole in the ground. But back then I wanted balance. A woman and a way to support her. A house and another house on the beach and a membership to a sports clubs. Kids. Now I realize you could have given me anything and I would have FUCKED IT ALL UP. All the things I needed and all the things I wanted. It was all bullshit. Old danny bullshit was never gonna change. For a little while I thought I could see light at the end of the tunnel. I needed to believe that. Things had gotten so bad. If I had to pick a time to plant a sign that said THIS IS THE BEGINNING OF THE END it would probably be Billys birth. Life starts with a slap in the face and his was no diferent. Thats why we slap babies because we gotta teach them how much life is gonna hurt. I looked down at the bloody skweeling thing and tried to smile but all I was thinking was NOW YOUR FUCKED DANNY. Nothing inside me was calm. It was all the same mess of broken faces and old ghosts. Nothing went away. Even GOD was egging me on. Telling me I was full of shit. Thats how it felt anyway. Now I can see I was crazy as a shithouse rat. The way I was acting. Especially with Sarah in those early days before she went sour. She was one of those beautiful young women with brains. The quiet ones who dont even know how pretty theyv become. All they can remember is being fat or pimply or skinny when they were kids. Those are the best ones. She had this pale delicate skin looked like the dust had never seen her. Like shed been living in a garden somewhere under a nice umbrella in the shade. I was tiptoying around her like a kid waiting to be yelled at. Hey shitheel stop touching the good china. But it was all part of my plan to get REVENGE on the world. To make something of myself and be something beter than my shity dad who was a mean old fucker. I wanted to be a hero and a champion. The working man who beat the rich. HA HA HA. What a joke. After I bought the house in Boca de Uchire things really stoped meaning anything. It was the last goal I had. After that all things were supposed to be good and I was gonna feel good with the world and my son and wife. But it was just a fucking mirage and ahead of me all I could see was dry dead sand with no end. So I gave up and tried to relax but it was impossible. Too hot in the sun and never enough drinks to cool danny down. After a few glasses of Whiskey Id feel decent for a bit and the thinking would be quieter but soon it would all come rushing back in the afternoon. Id be cracking in the sun like a piece of dry clay. Couldnt wet my mouth fast enough to stay drunk. So I started making strategys. Id spend as much time as possible with Sarah during my hours of soberness. Well sorta soberness. A few beers at least. Id get her to leave the baby and walk with me along the shore. Was like a dying man trying to enjoy his last moments on the earth. Didnt care about nothing. It was empty. Shed listen to the waves and look down at her toes cause she was so disapointed in me. She got more and more scared too. Wouldnt touch me during the day. I started spending lots of time at the beach house on the couch or alone watching the flamingoes fishing in the laguna. I didnt trust myself in the car for long distances neether so Id call Javier to make sure the gringos were still showing up. Yes sir he would tell me. Yes sir they still are. He was also disapointed. Id sober up for long enough to drive there once a month and collect the money. It was around then that Carlos first talked to me about the fertile fishing company. THOSE COCKSUCKERS. A couple of profesional gringos who droped by with their Venezuelan slaves to translate their bullshit into spanish. Trying to rope my boys into their gringo shit. Big black SUVS. Waving their MONEY around and telling my boys they were gonna buy the lake. Goverment aproved. Promising to hire Carlos and Javier and double their salarys. Giving them business cards. FULL OF SHIT EXPLOITERS. LIARS ALL OF THEM. Id never sell the fucking lake. It was MINE as long as I kept paying the mortgage. They couldnt do a FUCKING THING about it. They were just trying to put pressure on me and my boys. But I wasnt gonna crack. I should have paid Javier and Carlos better but life had become very expensive between the consolideted det and the babies and the Whiskey so I switched to Rum. Thats when the blackouts really started geting bad. It gives me the jiters just writing about the goddamn blackouts. But theres nothing to worry about really because theres NO BOOZE up here. I just gotta stay up here and never go down into the foothills. DONT GO DOWN INTO THE FOOTHILLS. Not that it would matter anymore. EVERYONE ABANDONED OLD DANNY

ANYWAYS. Fuck them all. The only things I need up here in the mountains are the things Im gona eat today and that stupid dog with his sad wite beard. Hes getting really old that one. Cant even keep up with me on the hikes through the mountain. He must be older than me. Even in dog years. And Im pretty fucking old.

Dengue Dreams (Age 7)

Lay her down and make her drink Coca Cola.

There's a thing got inside me, really pushed into my tummy. I squeezing down to make it stop but all it does is make me poo. When I poo, my butt burns and it spits strawberries. I'm always hot right now.

It wasn't me, it was Billy. I just sat and watched him do it, that's the truth.

It was alive and orange and hot. I think if this never stops in my tummy I'm gonna slice it open and rip out the hurt, like a pile of burning strawberries in my tummy. Mom's right here and it gets cold too, my toes knocking together and my teeth clacking. She tucks me into the blanket and I try closing my eyes. There's a hurt when I look at mom, so I keep my eyes up at the fan. She rubs my sides and I slap her fingers when my tummy makes me twist like a worm.

It's going to be alright, darling. You've got some fever. The doctor gave you some medicine but it takes a little while to work. You're being very brave. I'm impressed.

Her hands are cold on my burning forehead, and there's a Mommy soft and pretty.

Oh, Mommy.

I have *dengue* fever from the mosquitoes. They stick

their nose in you. So blood's filled with hurt, and the mosquito takes that. You can splat it on the wall and it'll be red. But the mosquito also gives bad, when it gives *dengue*. The jaina leads in too. It's close to the butt which is off limits for them if you're a lady, young lady. The Queen has no butt. She has manners, young lady, and she doesn't spit or pick her nose or put her elbows on the table. The Queen's in Mom like *dengue*'s in me. The Queen's got shiny spoons made of silver, white hair, and a red crown with sharp diamonds. Mom showed me a picture. She shows me pictures of England, where the Queen lives and Mom used to live.

I didn't do it. Billy played with the matches.

So why didn't you say anything?

I'm no tattle-tale.

Darling that was a long time ago. You're just feverish. Please try to drink some water. Just sit up for a moment and try to drink some water so you don't get dehydrated.

When I saw the curtains on fire I got scared of Billy. He was smiling when he did it.

There's no fire in the room, Abilena. That was years ago. Please try staying with me in reality. You're fine. I'm here to take care of you. You're sick. You're imagining things because you're having hallucinations from the *dengue*. None of it is real. But the medicine will help.

The little box was yellow and red and black. He took the matches and made the fire. Scratch, scratch, scratch, in his blue pajamas with the dinosaurs on it. He was looking at it but also looking through it. Devil eyes. Then the curtains got fire and Daddy came rushing cause I was crying.

You little imbecile.

But Billy, he just sat there, looking at the fire and looking through the fire, even when Daddy pulled his arm and smacked him

What I do wrong?

Abi. That fire wasn't your fault. It was nobody's fault.

Mom takes me to the toilet and rubs my belly when it burns and I push the sliding sand down my tummy. It's hurting my butt.

Abilena, you have to push a little. Once you go to the bathroom, your stomach won't hurt as much. Please make a little effort. Good job. That's a good job. Here. Stand so I can clean you up. There we go.

Mom carries me to bed, making goat sounds.

Would you like me to read you a book? I can read you the Princess and the pea. Once upon a time there was a Prince, and he wanted to find himself a Princess, but she must be a proper Princess.

I try looking at Mommy but I can't cause Daddy's fire's inside me. It wasn't just Billy lighting fires with the curtains. Daddy also makes fires with his cigarettes. I remember. There was a black dot on benjo's head. When I looked closer I could see the tick. He was brown with little hairs and his head was dipped into benjo. I patted benjo but didn't touch the tick. I don't like bugs, so. Scaredy-cat. I brought benjo to daddy. It's just a tick. He was sweet and his mouth was wet. So Daddy took his cigarette and held it between his fingers. See this? I nodded. Only way to remove a tick from a dog. You gotta burn the little fucker off. So I watched as Daddy pushed the cigarette into benjo and missed the black dot. Benjo yelped and yelped and Daddy held him and pulled the tick with his fingers. The tick exploded into blood and his head was still dipping into benjo. Next to the tick's head there was a brown pimple and curly hair where Daddy burned benjo. It smelled like the man's legs who jumped over the fire. Then benjo ran as fast as he could to join his gang. He was yelping and barking and didn't stop. Daddy looked at me sweet. See? I can see, Daddy. I can see you real good.

One evening there was a terrible storm; it lightened and thundered and the rain poured down; it was quite fearful. There came a knock at the town gate and the old King went off to open it.

Sometimes there's good yelping, but then it explodes in blood. He wiped the blood on his jeans and the yelping dogs are racing round and round. There's a racing gang of dogs here at the beach. All of them with their tongues hanging out of their mouths. I can see benjo and sammy and browny and the little ugly one. They're racing but the finish line isn't there.

You're feverish.

I swallow the Mom. I swallow where it hurts. What are those men doing? They're fighting. But they're hurting each other! The big metal box in the street and the first man pushes the other into it. You idiot, that's the point. The other man's face isn't a face, it's just a good yelp with plenty blood. From the school bus everybody watches as he hits and hits the other man. They're supposed to do that? Connie doesn't say nothing. Sometimes strawberries go rotten and they mush. The man's face is really red and he doesn't move. Then the bus keeps going to school. Still we all remembered the two men fighting in the street. One of them wasn't moving at the end. But there's no school, we just ride in circles and circles like we did for the School Run. That's the point. But I don't really get it. I just pretend to. Connie's plenty smart but she got real quiet when the other man stopped moving. It's supposed to have a finish line. If you don't go to school you won't never be a Lady. Nobody needs another stupid Lady. Mom says Queen says Lady.

Are you enjoying the story Abilena? Do you need to go to the bathroom again? It seems your fever's calmed. That's a good thing. I know you're still in pain, but you'll be fine. The doctor is very professional. I'll continue with the story. It was a Princess that was standing outside but gracious! What a figure she was with the rain and bad weather! The water ran all down her hair and her clothes and in at the toes of her shoes and out at the heels, and she said she was a real Princess.

The Queen sits in the box and watches the dogs go round and round with ticks in their head. In the middle of the dogs there's two men fighting and hitting. Next to the drink shack I'll stand and wait. Then I'll get what I like the most, a watermelon juice with ice. Oh and I remember when browny got her belly stuck on the fence. The fence was made of barbara wire. Then daddy found browny and helped her. He pulled a bit and then pulled real hard on browny and she turned inside out. She was like a cherry pie. Then browny was quiet and she ran away forever into the sky. She was still stuck to the barbara wire. God wants it that way. God knows. I asked mom about it. She said quiet down and eat your vegetables. Don't put your elbows on the table. How many times do I have to remind you? I can feel the race never ended. It just kept circling and barking.

Ah, we'll find that out right enough, thought the old Queen to herself, but she didn't say anything, she went into the bedroom, took all the clothes off the bed and laid one dried pea on the bottom of the bed. Then she took twenty mattresses and laid them on top of the pea, and then twenty eiderdowns on top of the mattresses, and there the Princess was to sleep that night.

The Queen was turned inside out and browny was winning the finish line. Things are quieter cause I'm in the room with Mom.

The story is almost over Abilena. Listen to this. Then they could see that she was a proper Princess, since she had felt the pea through twenty mattresses and twenty eiderdowns. Nobody could possibly have such tender skin but a real Princess. The girl was a real Princess, Abi!

She's holding my head and rubbing my hair and sobbing.

Abi, Abi, Abi. I don't know if I love him.

The light's orange and mom's sitting at the dinner table. Her face is a cherry pie and her mouth's a crust of bread nobody wants to eat. The white part's already eaten and daddy's not home yet. Mom's always waiting for daddy to come home. The watermelon juice is coming out of her eyes and mom tells me things about daddy. I don't know if I love him. He's out with the fishermen, mom, money doesn't grow on fucking trees. When you turn a fish inside out it's always full of money bills like a firework.

Boom! And Daddy throws water on the curtains.

Boom! Money bills on the beach.

Boom! You slice along the belly. Look. Look.

Boom! You pull the fishguts from here. Pinch them strong, Abi. Then pull them out. They're not for eating.

Boom! The dogs'll eat them. Then you can't kiss the

dogs no more, little Abi fishbreath. Little dog kisser. Yellow stainer.

Boom! Mom rubs and rubs but it's cutting my guts out, there's a hook that won't let go.

Boom! The *piraña* lives in the lake, not in the sea, you stupid little girl. *Estupida.*

Daddy's the boss. I don't know if I love him. Mom's sad but Daddy says pfff. Your mom. Always something with her. Always so dramatic.

Bill's in bed too. Can hear him breathing and see his eyeball shining in the dark. Downstairs the chairs make metal noises and mom and Dad are yelping good.

I don't know if I can do this anymore!

You keep fucking nagging me and I'm gonna lose my temper with you, Sarah!

Wet, wet, wet. I need to pee. I hold and hold and hold the balloon. Then it bursts warm and wet. Bill's asleep and I'm in the waves. I put my thumb in my mouth and tomorrow I'll be sick. Yellow stainer. Abilena.

Mom's cleaning me in the shower and I'm cold and shivering in the hot spray.

Your fever's coming down. The doctor says it's almost over. You've been yelling your head off.

But the finish line's never over. I sit on my butt and cry watermelons.

So the Prince took her as his wife, for now he knew that he had found himself a proper Princess, and the pea was put in the treasure chamber, where it is still to be seen, unless somebody has taken it away. Now there's a proper story for you.

It's over?

Yes, that's how the story ends.

I don't like the Queen. She made the Princess feel bad.

But it was for her own good.

Maybe.

Well you seem more awake at least.

Thanks for reading me the story, Mommy.

Daniel — 2 of June of 1997

Abilena was an angel who abandoned me. I cant never blame her though. Never. Shes too special for that. Like an angel coming down from the clouds to save danny but it was too late. I can see her perfect little face right now when I close my eyes. Makes me know I did it all wrong. Wish I could go back to those early days and change them. Make things different. Make beter choices from what I know now. Maybe I could have taken a diferent road. I was a robot making decisions without thinking. I was running on empty. Abilena was the only damn thing I did right when I put her into Sarah. When she was born I could tell she was from another place than the rest of us. Somewhere better. She had something inside her cherning out gladness. Always would and none of us could touch it. I knew she was gonna grow like a stuborn vine through the world always finding a path. It even sobered me! Sober danny with the fear of god in me. Id spend as much time with her as possible. Id follow them like a dog between Caracas and Boca de Uchire my wife and daughter. Sarah didnt trust me to hold the baby alone. She always wanted to make sure DANNY wouldnt drop little Bibi on her head. But I never woulda. DANNY BE CAREFUL DANNY. I held her like a preshous vaze and I NEVER drank too much around her. Abi put us together one last time before I puled us apart again with the booze. It must have been 65 almost 66. Leoni was president. That bald fuck had been LYING about infastructure and a new democracy. HA HA HA. Far as I could tell it just meant running big highways through the smaller lakes like mine. They wanted to buy me out but I wouldnt do it to Carlos and Javier. They had familys to feed. So I told Leoni to stick it up his ass. They ended up building around the lake close enough so the truck fumes would drift down to the water sometimes when trafick got busy. The sons of bitches were closing in on me with their machines. Private fishing corporations and government stooges. I was a fucking idiot to think there was a way to go back in time. Things were changing and the goverment was shitting the bed. But who cares about those FUCKING SCUM. Id rather piss up a tree than write about the politicos. Ive been having more visions like the one of Abilena in the crib. Their like seezures cracking through my brain. Sometimes they come when Im hiking with the dog whos still alive but barely. A memory will jump through the brown water like a fish. Ive been crying some. I feel ashamed of writing about it like Im not a man anymore but who gives a damn anyway. Up here in the mountains alone its different because a mans tears are just a drop of water in the mud. Didnt think Id ever write after last time. Its been a while. But it worked last time to get my brain calmer so maybe itll work again. Ive been going crazy without nobody else to talk to. Thinking maybe I dont exist. Wheres Abilena now? Does she ever think of me? Does anybody give a fuck about old danny? Shes happy to be rid of me I guess. Its because Im useless. If it werent for the dog Id off myself. But THE DOG needs me.

Sister and the Snakes (Age 11)

Thomaz was pulped in the propeller and spread out for the fishes. In the darker parts, after some slow sinking, the bits glowed red and pink with the floating jellyfish. For many moments the dust was still, shining like stars in the black water. Then the barracuda came fast and long, snapping up the chunks with their long skinny teeth and turning for more. When I woke I was covered in sweat, and I asked Mom if I could call Thomaz. Nonsense, she said, it was just a dream. But it wasn't just a dream.

Daddy's new boat is made of white plastic with no stains. He wears a captain's hat and holds the steering wheel with one hand, drinking cocktails with the other. I sit on the rough white plastic with Bill. Mom's on the other side, arm over the cooler and smiling.

It's so nice to have you all in one place. It happens so rarely now that you're a university student, William.

The big buzz of the motor makes everything shake. The pushing's happening under my belly, the new pushing I never recognized before. Now it's there, for the last few days, and the motorbuzz is making me tingle and swell. It feels like a fruit sitting in water, pushing out past its own skin to feel a bit more.

Dreams are wild and black when I'm tired, and I've been tired. Can't sleep properly since a couple days. When I stand there's something pulling at me, like I'm being pulled by the earth and the dirt, and he wants something from me. The earth is a he but god doesn't know. The earth is a she, with her tangle of dirt and strange plants.

Last night the moon was full as it gets. Dad was drinking beer in front of the *casita* with Bill, who's a man now. He answers back and everything. Mom was reading in her big wicker chair. I stood in the doorway and that's when I felt it, the hungry earth and its dry need. The moon was alive too, speaking to my belly somehow, shining instructions through the darkness.

Between us on the boat, a sliced barracuda. Dad caught it earlier and slammed its head on the plastic before chopping it up. He squirted lemon all over the slices and now there's blood and lemon everywhere. I try to eat a piece but feel wobbly and sick. Mom looks but doesn't touch it. Bill eats a few pieces and drinks beer like a man. Dad smiles and stares ahead of us into the ocean blue. Then I notice on the outside skin of my private parts, a slow creeping water. The smell of fish is strong with the cutting lemon. Trickling out from under my left leg, a small snake of pink water's making it's path through the rough white plastic. A second snake and a third. I'm sitting on a chopped fish but I can't tell anyone. Soon the snakes swerve right and trickle down through the wooden floor, down into where the water pools. I don't say anything. I'm a sliced fish. Thank god Dad's still staring ahead and Bill's now standing at the back of the boat, looking out into the foam. Mom's across from me, noticing the snakes and smiling for some reason. She stands up and stumbles towards me to punish me. But then she doesn't cause she uses a towel to soak the pink trickle and makes me stand up to wipe my butt like a baby. Then she takes the pink towel and puts it under me.

Sit down. It's ok. You're a lady now.

I'm a cut lady with a slice of fish where I bleed onto the towel. I look at my secret Mom and she's smiling like a whisper. Bill's sitting next to me drinking beer. His hair's orange and his skin is covered in freckles. His chest's bony and it pokes out in ribs. Dad's a brown captain and Mom's a smiling stupid. I stay quiet and make sure the towel doesn't move. If my blood gets into the ocean the barracuda will smell it for miles and chew me to death. God doesn't know. That's not for me. But the girls at school did talk. A cut that never stops. The motorbuzzing makes it tingle inside my private parts.

Of course it's that. I can feel the sharp hooks on both sides, coming and going in waves. They talk about it at school. Mom smiles. Nothing's cut. The dead barracuda's smiling needles, all chopped up and bleeding in the middle.

I haven't told Mom, but I'll never be a lady. I want to be a woman like Janis Joplin when she smiles.

We dock and Mom wraps the towel around my waist and nobody notices the warm blood running down my leg, sucked by the dirt and crawling through the sand.

It's a bright night and the moon's pushing hard inside me. Dad and Bill are in front of the *casita*, half-asleep and gurgling sweetly in the firelight.

Mom shows me how to push in the tampon and make the walls feel. There's a path inside me, and there's never not gonna be. I'm a woman in the bathroom, and I'll always be a woman.

Are your nipples swollen?

I take off my t-shirt and Mom touches them, smiling.

Everything's right, Abilena. It's early but everything's right. We're sisters now.

I hold Mom around her fatness. Last night I heard her in the kitchen with no lights on. She was eating *platanitos* and drinking pepsi. There was just the sound of crumpled plastic and gurgling in the dark kitchen, eating desperate like dogscraps. Now she's my sister but she'll always be my Mom.

When the moon's high and cloudless, the phone rings and Mom answers it. Her eyes are wide open circles.

Oh. Ok. Oh my god. I'm so sorry. Oh Jesus. I'm... Well if you need anything... ok. Alright. Good night. I... Abi. Abilena.

Yes?

That was Thomaz's mother. He's... Abi, he's been in a boating accident. It's awful. Something happened to him. Something awful. No, Abi, don't cry. Your father can't know tonight. He can't know. Keep your tears, Abi. Thomaz is free now. He's with god.

But I know he's not, cause I know where he is.

Sarah — March 9th, 1996

AFFIRMATIONS
I will focus on remembering my past.
I will not gossip or cause discord in the community.
I understand that my actions have caused discord in the community.
I ask for God's forgiveness.

I didn't know it back in university, but I would never set foot on European soil again. Within three years I finished my bachelor's degree in sociology and gave birth to William, and within a few more to Abilena. We settled in *El Peñon,* an upscale neighborhood of expatriates and traveled Venezuelans. The house was built right into the hillside on two levels, with a gorgeous second story: kitchen, living room, dining room, and a balcony giving onto the garden. Of course the white marble staircase turned out to be fake, but who could tell the difference? One of my only qualms: the dimness of the bottom floor. It was a basement of sorts, and all the bedrooms led to this unfortunate little "foyer" (a bit of a stretch). There was even a metal door in that room, and it gave onto a dismal "veranda" (more like a *cul-de-sac*). But I made do, of course, by turning it into a television room.

AFFIRMATIONS
I am grateful for the home I was given.
I understand it was a God-given privilege.
I am on a spiritual path.

Daniel seemed obsessed with keeping me safe at the

time, and argued that the Caracas Sports Club would offer me an active social life. It would also keep me safe from the criminals and the good-for-nothings while he left on his trips and tended to his flourishing fishing business. It was all to feed the family, he explained.

AFFIRMATIONS
I can see my husband's best intentions.
I understand he is a child of God.
In my heart I find forgiveness for his sins.

The Caracas Sports Club was an expansive piece of land with several sporting fields, terraces, pavilions, and squash courts. It was a leisurely and safe place to raise children. I could sit safely in a deck chair and look at *El Avila*, the national park to the north of Caracas, a place so massive, mountainous, and wild it always seemed on the verge of spilling down into the city and overtaking civilization. Its mist-ringed peaks were so beautiful. Sometimes they filled me with unexplainable sadness. A deep emptiness

AFFIRMATIONS
I can see now I was given gifts by God.
I am finding out the truth about my life.
The sisters are here to guide me.

Two Billies (Age 12)

When there's too many wasps, I can't even go there. They feast in the shadows on the dried *frescolita*, pink and sticky on the soda pop rims and red metal tables. A wasp'll sting you over and over cause it doesn't die nobly like a bee. The workers don't even seem to mind, their calm brown faces always very still in the shade of the club's cafeteria. I like all the bad stuff, like *tequeños* and *empanadas* but not with shark meat or anything fishy. Mom likes even worse things, like *platanitos* and ruffles and ice-cream, but only at night. During the day she sips juices and doesn't touch food. Like a whale by the swimming pool, *la ballena* of the sports club, the little kids call her, and giggle as they run around.

I wrestle them all and shove them off the swimming pool bridge, the little shits. I'll twist their goddamn arms off. I'll drown them in the pool. Try saying it to my face, you little turds.

Con queso always gives me oil and I soak the paper under the tap and wipe my face with it. Then I lift my shirt to check and I have them, for all to notice, but I'll never be fat. All the boys care about is titties, but they won't touch what's mine. I'll wrestle those little shits into the pool and hold them under til they swallow water.

I like the nights best, when the lamps come on and the buzzing starts. The paths are dark and splotched with rotten mangoes. Even though it's cold, at night my blood gets warmer like a cat's. I can creep around the club and explore what's not too dark. I'll run between the pools of light, past trees and their long drooping vines, under the swarms pressed to the bulbs, across the paths paved rough with sticky black tar, still hot from the day's sun.

Out in the real world, dad says there's lots of problems. It's not just wasps. Uncle Gerald got his face blown through by a bullet, just sitting at a stoplight, just for some *bolos*. What's the world coming to.

Mr.Novitski says it's cause of history, what the Europeans and the Americans did to the Indians and the Colored People and how it got this way. Dad says that stupid fuck Herrera couldn't find his asshole with a flashlight. Worst president since the last three, he always jokes.

You don't live in the real world, Abilena. You're a spoiled brat. That's why there's armed men guarding your school gates. To keep your expat bubble safe, you little idiot. You don't know a goddamn thing about what's happening.

Dad smells like rum and I want to push him over the balcony and down the long steep grass so he tumbles and hits his head on the avocado tree. Mom says nothing and doesn't eat. She sips her juice and tells us to relax. But nobody ever relaxes and Bill just leaves the table and takes his motorcycle to his friend Ernesto's. Most of the time they hang out there, but sometimes they come over to the house, especially when mom and dad are gone.

When Ernesto looks at me, he's there. I can feel him, and sometimes I need to fold up and get away from his eyes. He likes to use his black eyebrows in a friendly way, pushing and pushing without saying anything. Just standing there. Bill notices but doesn't notice. When the men look, they're always with you, taking up space. They stare right down the path, making the walls feel. Sometimes unwelcome. Ernesto walks wide and makes dumb faces. He's got a big nose and always raises one bushy eyebrow to call me bibi.

They're all the same. Connie's face is scrunched and sharp like a pack of pencils when she tells me that. You know what they want. She whispers the word like it's real bad. Pussy. I don't like Connie. She knows a lot of things, but I can't be sure about any of them. Plus the party found out where she did it. In the bathroom like a slut. There was a boy with Connie in the bathroom at the party, and Connie was puking cause she drank too much punch. It was that boy Camilo, the one who takes medecine when he drinks and got caught by Jacky's parents. Hes' not at school anymore. I was standing in the hallway when he left the bathroom and Connie didn't come out. So then JC slapped Camilo on the back and replaced him in the bathroom with Connie. Later she came out with JC but everybody already knew.

It's nice that Connie's a slut, cause then I don't have to go bad. I can be good so nobody ever touches me like that. I told Susan and she told the rest of the class. Connie shouldn't come to eighth grade parties. She's older. She's in ninth grade but she should be in tenth grade. She repeated a year. So I told her maybe with you, but not with me. I'm basically a good girl if I'm popular. Got four valentines delivered to the classroom and they were all from good boys.

Ernesto isn't too short either. He's not in any grade. He's a college kid who even works now that he finished school. So Connie can talk all she wants, cause she's got no friends anyway. Nobody likes her and it makes sense. It's not my fault, cause I didn't do it with two boys in the bathroom. Fuck Connie.

Sometimes Ernesto goes to the bathroom with Bill and when they come out they're always nice. Ernesto calls me bibi but he doesn't push, just sits with a big dumb grin and lets his eyebrows relax. Like a coca cola. Yeah, just like a coca cola. Like a diet coke. And they laugh and laugh, being nice with his little sister for once. Bill sits in his room usually, brooding and pouting. Mom always says that.

Will you please stop brooding and pouting, William, and come join your family for some quality time.

But he doesn't do it and his room always smells funny. There's a black mountain round Billy, and on the side of the mountain there's lots of jungle trees and giant billboards for Belmont cigarettes where everybody's smiling and playing beach ball. Billy likes to paint their eyes black and draw a moustache on the girls. He doesn't have a girlfriend. He looks like he's sick. But when he sits with Ernesto his eyes have little fires in them and he smiles again, like he used to. Then he gets nice and calls me *pequeña*, putting his arm round my shoulder.

There's two Billies. One's my brother and the other's a black mountain.

Sarah — March 12th, 1996

I'll rip this page out of the book when I'm done writing about that cow. I'll chew it into little bits and flush it down the toilet so they never find it and humiliate me again. I know Anna-Felicia has been making comments to Carla about my toilet cleaning because she takes pleasure in watching her reprimand me.

Dear God, I struggle to please you every day. Please explain what purpose you have for placing this woman in my life? She's like a mosquito.

There's no way to avoid what I'm feeling and there's nobody I can speak to here. These women just repeat themselves over and over. They tell me I have a lot to learn and that I should be patient. But they are all underhanded and vicious. Well, maybe not all of them. Mainly A-F. Maybe only A-F.

I just feel alone. I miss my babies. I wonder where they are right now.

Is it too late to go back, God?

The sisters want me to be as thorough as possible, but it's difficult to remember the exact order of events. What disappeared first, my beauty or his touch? I will list what I can remember and trust God with the rest.

Daniel stopped touching me. I gained an incredible amount of weight. He grew distant and increasingly paranoid, claiming several political groups were plotting against him. One night he returned home very late from his monthly visit to the fishing lake. He was beside himself, screaming at the top of his lungs and pacing the balcony, waking the children with his delusional ranting. He claimed a car filled with masked men had tried to run him off the road. He was swearing like a madman. I implored him to watch his language in front of our children, but it was a lost cause. He was completely out of control.

AFFIRMATIONS
I am grateful for

I believed in the sanctity of marriage. I never would have left him. How could I? He was the father of my children. I had no way of supporting myself. I had a worthless undergraduate degree in sociology and no work experience whatsoever. I was too ashamed to contact my family. What would I have told them anyway? That my entire life had become a lie? That I no longer recognized the man I married? To do what? Impose on my doddering parents in their twilight years? I would never dare. And what about the children? So I absconded into an endless succession of deck chairs, movie nights, and bridge games. I became a sow slowly roasting over the coals of my expired marriage.

AFFIRMATIONS
This is the body I was given by God.
I am grateful
RUFFLES (ONION AND SOUR CREAM)
RUFFLES (PLAIN SALTED)

COCA COLA (DIET)
PLATANITOS
CONDENSED MILK
COFFEE
BREAKFAST TEA
MUG
SPOON
ELECTRIC KETTLE?
MILK CHOCOLATE (NESTLE)
WHITE CHOCOLATE (NESTLE)
SUGAR
~~PANCAKE MIX (AUNT JEMIMA'S)?~~
~~MAPLE SYRUP (AUNT JEMIMA'S)?~~
~~FRYING PAN?~~
OH KEEP DREAMING SWEETHEART
keep dreaming

The Red Heron (Age 12)

Even Dad doesn't cut his nails cause you need them long to peel the shrimp. Inside them there's shit, always. You can try to clean it out but it never really works, just smears into the pink flesh and we're gonna eat shit all summer. The laguna's wide and flat with murky swarming waters. There's green and brown plants living in there with the shrimp and the fish, and green stems pushing from the water to grow their delicate leaves, no white sand to stand on, and no salt in the water to clean it. Just a filth of mud and rot, and the shrimp born blind in the flat unmoving waters, their little black eyes caked with beach soil, born to be caught by the beautiful flamingos.

God found the flamingo too beautiful and pushed her neck into a twist. God made Bill twisted and red, and the flamingo also has sad green eyes. The flamingo never lets the water touch her. To make sure of it, she grows long pink legs made of leather, and you'll never see a flamingo with a filthy belly. The only bad part of the flamingo is her mouth. When she gets hungry, she has to dip her nose into the mud and dig for shrimp. She does a little dance, poking her feet up and down in disgust when her head's underwater. So the flamingo has a black mouth, but that's only cause she doesn't want to starve. To be honest, the only reason the flamingo even stands in the laguna is that she gets hungry. And every evening the flamingos poke their feet up and down and flap their giant wings, shedding the mud as they take off for Bonaire. Bonaire's the island where all the flamingos live, a place without mud. Their long thin legs look funny when they fly, flapping uselessly in the wind. Flamingos are long and beautiful, and when they fly into the sunset I often think of Bill. He doesn't come to the beach any more. He's got no use for us. I think Bill was born to fly with the flamingos, but he never got wings. His eyes are green with hunger and his skin's white with anger. Bill's a dead flamingo that was never born. When I make some money I'll buy him a ticket to Bonaire and he can clean his filthy belly.

Connie told me her mother's an alcoholic. She told me an alcoholic's a Dad who drinks too much and never stops. I've seen them living under the bridges on the highway, their noses all blown up and gross. Thank god Daddy's nose is still strong. He only drinks cause he's been to war, defending his country from the Korean Communists who wanted him dead. He never killed anybody, just used his rifle to point the gun and stay clean from all the trouble.

I'm wearing my new bikini and walking on the white sand, looking down at the shoreline for rotten fish and their bony spikes.

I don't look like you, mom, cause you're fat. I'll never be like you. But I don't say that, of course.

The boys look at me on the beach, the fishermen boys with their grey eyes, brown skin covered in dried salt, pulling nets onto boats and pulling boats ashore and flipping them with their strong veins. Sometimes they take naps under the overturned boats til their fathers come to wake them. In the wet shade it must smell like steaming fish and rotten wood. The wood's chipped on the boats, scraped by the sand, fingernails long enough to peel the shrimp. Waves crash at the dip, carving at the sand and pulling babies out to sea. I've heard it told. I believe it.

I've never said this to anyone, but when I was out there once I almost stayed for good. The pull was too much and my arms and legs stopped working. There was nobody on the beach to hear me. I was alone in the green blue. I got pulled and pulled til I just stopped struggling. Held my breath one last time and let it take me. I was at the bottom for who knows how long, lying on the sand. They say the sand's a spit. It lives between the lake and the ocean. Drifting on the spit, I could tell everything was gonna be quiet. I even liked it. Then my lungs thought about the *piraña* fish and the barracuda fish and the long white needles. How my flesh would be floating in bits, and I thought about the red heron. He lives with the flamingo, making sure nobody breaks a leg. When the flamingo breaks her leg, she falls into the mud and flaps to tell the heron. He calls everybody and they deliver the flamingo of its flesh, making it part of the laguna. So the white shrimp make the flamingo pink and the pink flamingo make the heron red and the red heron flies low and long, skimming the bloody water as he takes off for Bonaire.

Then I see it on the sand, a blue watch with long thin dials. It's lying there with the driftwood and algae, still ticking. I hold it in my palm and check for water. Swatch. Seven thirty-four PM, but it's not. It's probably one PM here, and lunch's at two. My name was supposed to be Abilene, mom told me, but the office wouldn't let them. They said you must pick from this list. Mom found Abilena on the list and got it for me. One day Abilene will take off and fly to London or Paris and give birth to a son. I'll call him Adrian and he'll never peel any goddamn shrimp. I strap the watch to my wrist like a promise.

Abilena sees the entrance of the old compound, every summer's compound, and she lies in a hammock strung between two coconut palms. She looks at the watch and listens to the seconds tick. Everything goes by ticks. One day Browny was bit by a coral snake in the pink part of her mouth. I was there and I saw it happen too. There was a flash of red and black and yellow and Browny yelped. Then the snake was gone into the bushes. At first things were fine, but then Browny couldn't yelp. She lay down and gave up at the bottom of the spit. It's just the waves. The big ones. Then it's hard to be wanting. Because in the end Janis died with a cigarette in her hand, wedged against the bedside table, nose smashed on the carpet.

Daniel — 24 of July of 1997

The rains have been lite this year and some of the plants are turning brown. The dog sleeps indoor a lot on account of the humidity. Seems to be tiring the old fucker. I dont care much but sometimes I get lonely on the hikes without his running around. Can feel my bones grinding in their meat too. Thats what happens to most old people. Im nothing special. I guess its kinda nice not having any distractions when youre busy dying. The storys coming to me clearer in chunks and pieces. Even though Id rather not I remember the weekend Javier drowned in the lake. I spent it with THE FAMILY speeding around the Boca de Uchire coast in the new boat I COULDNT AFORD. Even poured the Rum into cocktails and took the day off from the bottle if you know what I mean. 25 HP Johnson reved all the way up so it was splitting the water like a tunelling fish. I have this clear image of looking back at my wife and son and daughter and it seemed like things were at their best. Even god sometimes gives me a day off is what I thought. Even Sarah was in a good mood about me. But of course Billy was pouting like he did all the fucking time. That boy was complicated. Tried all the different ways to get along with him. Had a sort of sorry spirit in him. Was the oposite of Abilena. But I know I did lots of bad things to him. Some I remember and some I dont. Of course he never made it easy. When I tried to to talk to him hed always snap at me like a goddamn crocodile. Made me want to beat the daylites out of him. I did FEED him. I did CLOTHE him. I did send the boy to PRIVATE SCHOOLS nobody sent me to. But there was just something eating him. I guess the apple never falls far from the tree. When he finally stood up for himself and lost his cool it actualy felt pretty good. Then at least I knew what I was dealing with instead of all the pouting and creeping around with the DRUGS. Thats one of the things ruining this country. All the narcotraficantes making the kids crazy. Conio old man what about Javier. Well he drowned right there in front of those gringos. Must have been drunker than hell. Guess I wasnt the only one with problems at home. Carlos told me all this on the phone. Javiers wife had caught him with a younger girl fooling around close to home. Thats the mistake! NEVER close to home. No matter how it happened really but she was making life hell for him of course. WOMEN. Didnt tell the kids but held it over his head instead. When a man cant have the basics things. We need FREEDOM. Specially a simple man like Javier. So he was coming drunk to work. Nothing new under the sun. No big deal. A drunk venezolano motoring the gringos around the lake. They probably thought it was funny and anyway they were always drunk too. But he got so plastered one day that he fell right over into the water. I dont think he slept all night on account of his wife bothering him about what hed done. So he falls right into the water and cant remember how to swim hes so gone. Before the gringos even knew what was happening hed already hit the bottom. Dont know how he did it cause if you have air in your lungs youd float. Maybe they were full of booze. Maybe he had a heart attack. The gringos probably thought it was a prank he pulled on foreners. After a few minutes of laughing they saw he wasnt coming back up. They started figuring he might not be joking after all. Had to handle the boat themselves and motor back to shore and tell Carlos. They left all their fish with him and a huge tip on top of it. Thousands of dollars in blood money. So Carlos called me. I was in a great mood at the time. Drinking beer in front of the beach house after a day out on the sea. But the bad news really hit me in the guts. After that Carlos brought his brother and son to work with him. Basically ran the busines himself. He wouldnt touch Javiers money. I ofered it many times. He knew it was dirtier than hell. I wouldna either. But I needed it. Funny thing is that Javiers clothes came back up from the bottom. The lake shucked him outta them like a slippery corncob. And he musta stayed down there I guess. Who the fuck knows.

Los Hombres Guapos (Age 13)

Her wicker throne's in the betamax room, which mom calls the foyer. Each tape's labeled by hand with the name of the movie she copied. Ladies come by to pick them up or return them, and she takes their *bolos* and stuffs them into a shoebox. She spends most of it on snacks. Mom's the tired old queen of Caracas expats. Most nights they sit upstairs around the glass table playing bridge and drinking cocktails. Then she brings ladies down into the betamax room and they stare up at the stacks, squinting to read the titles in the yellow light.

Just down the hall is Bill's room, where I found a group of ants feasting on an old apple core under the bed. It was just a cloud of ants in the shape of an apple core really, with a trail leading out the window so they could carry the bits. Bill's surfboard was in his closet the whole time. I guess he was the thief. I went through his senior yearbook and they used a big picture of him on his page. Even Ernesto managed to write something, thanking his family and friends for blah, blah, blah. He chose his own picture too. Holding a pool cue and looking up at the camera, leaning into the shot, big eyebrows making sure you're safe. But Billy's picture, well it's just an enlarged version of his school headshot, blurry and sad. He looks into the camera with exhausted certainty, eyes grey, face grey, hair grey. Back then they hadn't invented color yet, so everybody was just black and grey. Sometimes I sleep in his bed cause it still smells of him and I miss my brother Billy.

Told Connie I was sorry about what I did. She just looked at me, smiling, like she already knew it. Now we're friends. Some of the other girls aren't too happy about it though, cause they really hate Connie and talk about her all the time. But I don't care much about that, cause my skin's too bad to be popular most weeks.

Mostly I sit in the art room with Miss Mendoza, painting things pink and waiting for ninth grade to end. I painted the pencil sharpener. I painted the garbage can. I painted a whole chair. That took a few weeks cause I wanted to get it right. Didn't want any wood or metal to shine through. I was looking for that pure pink, the kind that shines like a cartoon. Like the pink panther.

Connie's been telling me about her things. I'm a good girl so I listen carefully but don't say much, which is ok cause she loves talking. Right now she's telling me about orgasms and I'm painting a broken television in the art room. We both have study hall and Miss Mendoza likes us, so we can usually stay here as long as we want. If we don't get too loud.

Miss Mendoza's editing a movie about her ex-husband. She does installation art about suicide. Got a shaved head and smiles all the time. She's better than most teachers.

The front one's a lot less intense. It's still cool, and it's easier to make alone. The longer you go in circles, pushing it, the more it'll happen. It blows up in your cunt and tingles all the way down to your toes. You can feel it in your whole body a little bit, but it's mostly in the bottom part. *Debajo.*

I look at Connie and think about the mosquitoes.

You should try it sometime, Abi, it's totally worth it.

Maybe.

I can't believe you've never had one. They're the best.

Keep it down, Connie, she's gonna hear us.

Miss Mendoza? Are you kidding me? She definitely jerks off. She's got an ex-husband. I bet they fucked all the time. She probably invented the back one.

The back one?

Yes. Behind the wall, there's another part. If you curl back there, it's kinda rough. The best way's to use a boy.

Connie, you're horrible.

Oh come on Abi, I get it. But you can't always be in love. Sometimes it's just for fun. They can be like... things.

Aren't you scared of becoming. Um. Aren't you scared of giving too much?

You're such an idiot sometimes.

Just because you

Shut up and listen to me. You've already lost everything, Abi. It's already gone. You just haven't realized it yet. So don't spend your whole life trying to be clean, cause you're gonna lose that game. Just act like you're already dirty and you'll feel better. Don't pay attention to what people think, ok?

Ok. Stop yelling.

So do you wanna hear about the back one?

Alright, tell me about the back one, but keep it down for god's sake.

So the back one can happen if the boy's been poking at it for a while. It's like a sponge or a sea cucumber.

Gross.

If you squish it over and over, then it's like your heart's connected and you can feel the blood pumping. Then something super weird happens, cause you feel like you wanna pee. The first time it happened, I told him to stop, cause I thought I was gonna piss all over him.

Girls, quiet down. Quit laughing like goddamn hyenas. I'm trying to work.

Sorry, Miss Mendoza. Won't ever happen again, swear to god.

That's a lie, Connie, and you know it.

We love you Miss Mendoza!

I guess someone has to. But if you keep having fun I'll never get any work done and you'll both drop out of school and I'll get fired and we'll end up pregnant in a shack in *La Vega*.

So you pee?

No, you don't. It just feels like it. But you have to keep going. Then there's an earthquake that explodes and shoots into your skull and fingers and down into your toes. It keeps coming and coming, and your whole body shakes like crazy.

That sounds awful, Connie. It sounds like... what's that thing... epilepsy. An epileptic seizure.

Well it's not. It's great. One day you'll understand.

Maybe it only works for you. Maybe you're a weirdo.

Maybe.

I paint Connie's knee pink and she smacks me. Miss Mendoza comes over and pretends to be angry with us. Then we sit in her office and watch the video about her ex-husband, who's an asshole and a jerk. Miss Mendoza deserves better, but she doesn't need a man anyway. Even dad's rotten in the roots.

Two weeks ago I sat in the kitchen with mom and she told me everything. Your father never went to war, honey. He made it up. You fat bitch, I thought. Then why did he tell me that? Well, Abi, sometimes he likes to tell stories. Jesus. So dad's a fucking liar? Well... he exaggerates. And stop swearing in front of your mother.

But I don't tell Connie or Miss Mendoza about dad's lies, cause Miss Mendoza's gonna be the driver when we escape down the coast to Georgetown and live in Guyana on a ranch with no men.

When I get home I can tell something's weird. Nobody's playing bridge and most of the lights are off. I tiptoe down the stairs and mom's in the betamax room, sitting on the throne and watching Indiana Jones.

He's such a handsome man, isn't he Abi?

Hi mom.

Hello my darling. Could you be a dear and fetch me my slippers? There's a draft and I'm freezing my toes off.

Sure. Where are they?

They're in my room.

Where's dad?

He's in Bill's room.

Why?

Because they're having a conversation between men, what do I know? I'm just an old lady with no slippers.

I walk the speckled marble with cold feet, past the bedroom door, through which I can hear the men talking, and I stop for a moment and look at the poster of Lynne Boyer, the woman who won the world twice on her surfboard, but all I can make out are murmurs, and anyways it's not right to listen, so I keep walking down the hall. The parents' room smells warm and awful, like rotten avocadoes. I hold my nose and get out fast. Mom's pink and purple feet are dangling from the red velvet as I push the slippers on.

Thank you darling, you're wonderful.

I kiss her forehead. She tastes of foundation, eyes fixed on the screen, frozen in the blue glow.

I love you, mom.

Her eyes leave the screen for a moment and there's a face inside the face, cause Mom's beautiful when I see her. She did it all for me.

I love you too, Abi.

Her eyes bounce back and forth.

Would you like to watch Harrison Ford with me?

No thanks, mama.

But I sit on her lap anyway, careful not to crush her legs with my bony butt. In the movie Indiana Jones is running from a big boulder. He escapes. After a few minutes I can hear the men arguing loudly in Billy's room and I no longer pay attention to the movie. Their voices start shaking the wood and I stare at the door. Suddenly a foot appears. It shoots through the door, splintering the wood in all directions, and I recognize Bill's Chuck Taylor, black and white with worn-out soles. His jeans are rolled up and I can see his scraped calf. Then the foot disappears back into the hole and there's a moment of silence before the door comes down and oh my god, they're gonna kill each other. Dad's on the ground and Bill's holding his neck, baggy white shirt splattered brown, skin red from the neck up, eyes fixed in a lifeless trance.

Two men standing now, collar-gripped and pulling each other into the betamax room. A quiet, strained dance around mom. She's trembling like a big jello cake when the tapes start falling. The sound of music. Star wars. The godfather. A clatter of plastic shards. One flew over the cuckoo's nest. Apocalypse now. Chinatown. Mom's crying now, choked into her fat neck, and the two men crush movies under their feet as they punch and slam each other into the shelves. Casablanca. Vertigo. Some like it hot. Dad's killing Billy in the movies. Mom's watching the scary parts, she doesn't shield her eyes with a box of popcorn or hold my hand til it hurts. That man. Such a handsome man.

I stood and watched the same way Connie watched from the school bus that day. The two men in the street. It didn't end well. Connie didn't say nothing. She just stared out the window silently. Did he kill that guy? I don't know. Did he kill him? I said I don't know. Connie. Leave me alone, Abi. Connie, Connie. Just leave me alone, you little moron.

Mom's still sitting when they stop. Billy's caught in the slanting light, propped against the stairs, breathing hard. Dad's crouched in the black plastic, a panting bull surrounded by shattered betamaxes. Blood on the walls like spots of black light shining from an unseen disco ball. Blood running like mascara tears down mom's face.

And that's how mom wasn't the queen of the expats anymore. She didn't say anything, just took a long bath and went to bed. The next day she started eating meals again. No more juices. And she found god.

Sarah — March 16th, 1996

I often cry while performing my chores around the center. The sisters tell me it's normal, that they all underwent the same emotional turmoil upon arrival. Claudia, bless her heart, told me: "Through persistent practice your heart will remember how to radiate God's grace and with time He will overwhelm you with His calm."

Still, I find it difficult to believe my constant tears don't speak poorly of my character. Just as many sisters before me, I have now been entrusted with the hand washing of all robes, towels, and bedding for the center. It's this basic manual labor that supposedly bespeaks my service to God. But nary a piece is folded and returned to the wooden wardrobes without a tear having grazed its surface. In this way sorrow touches all my life's worthy endeavours.

During my silent prayers, I find myself assailed by horrifying scenes from the past. Then some sweet memory will emerge like a golden chalice from the ruins: Abilena's face, tender and childish; or Daniel's strong, loving embrace in those early days. I cling pathetically to these pleasant remembrances as I'm forced to continue trudging through the wreckage of bygone days.

AFFIRMATIONS:
I recognize my inability to perceive my own progress.
I trust the judgment of others.
The sisters are here to guide me.
~~I am not alone.~~

He Plays Field Hockey (Age 16)

The crabgrass rolls thick and sharp til the base of the cliff. Then it's just a dry crumble of dirt rising steep behind the bruised treeline. If you climb to the top there's the wet green valley where he uses his teeth, shoes jammed with black mud, chewing my lip and tasting the blood. Feel it most when the night falls, swelling and beating and running the path as they finish hockey practice. I picture him wrapping the stick with ripped cloth and tapping his palm to test the weight.

He'll chew my clothes off and put his cold salty tongue where the heat's got nowhere to go. He better tear them to pieces out there. I bleed when Connie bleeds when Miss Mendoza bleeds when the moon's full. Connie says take what you want today cause you might not want it tomorrow, and you'll be a day closer to death. A day closer to my tits drooping and my cunt drying up and my hair going out. But tonight I'm on fire like a house burning to bits, family photos and all.

You fucking coward. You sniffling coward, you.

I take him sweating from the hockey field and drag him to the top. We stand still in the heavy air, breathing with each other. I can tell there's nothing anyone could ever do. The rivers'll push through the earth and the trees'll thrust from the soil and the teeth'll chew it all, right down to the naked bone. There's no need to worry.

I shove Ernesto and we tumble the slope, leaping the

fallen trunks and crushing the seedlings to mud.

Abi. Abi.

Shut up.

But.

Shut up. Keep going.

The trunks're tall twisted vines sealed by ancient oozing sap. I'm gonna find that cold pool of salt to dip my heat in. I'm gonna swim in the ashen river and let the waters carry through. He's gonna lie on the mossy log and let the birds cry out to the insects and the insects cry out to god.

Abi.

Take it off.

Eyes frightened at first, then clear and still and hard. I close on him like an anemone, gripping the push and screaming from the canopy. When they cut the fish they do it quick, white and bloodless. His eyes stay open, frozen and unblinking. You can never tell until you. You can never. But the sound he making. But the sound. There's a forever in. There's a never.

Abilena. Abilena. I could just die. I could just lie down and die, Abi.

I've wanted you forever. You're my never. I could just.

Jam it down into the mud, into the bloody muddy sludge. Let the knife fall into the cold hard grass and sink to the hilt.

Ernesto, you fill me like a knife fills a wound.

There's the mud-spattered face of the boy I. There's the mud spattered. Oh boy. You can't find out until you find out. The green's no peace under the rain, more like a ragged splitting push, like a rotten log as it falls. Spit up the night in every moment that we. You'll know when you finally know. Then the stars like sores and the wind like a tongue, running you whole, lashing water to rock. Beating rotten in the perfect center. Two bodies torn and chewed up by the rough bark.

Abilena. Abilena.

There's plenty stars out, between the leaves, and we lie on our backs, holding hands. I'm no virgin forever.

Abi, say something Abi. Please say something.

But I don't say nothing.

Daniel — 28 of July of 1997

Today a memory hit me like a thunderbolt. I was hiking with the dog somewhere between Little Hell and Mouth of the Tiger. It was a vision but it felt real. Like a halucination on LSD. Had to sit on a rock to get steady again. Even now I can see her skwinting as she looked up at me to ask the question. Are we poor Daddy? So I told her no Bibi were not poor. I can remember everything she said that day and the way she had white sunscreen smeered on her nose. I remember the trees born with no leaves in the lake. The raw wood was growing like a few black hairs from a bald mans head. It was just the two of us sitting in the boat with our rods. Who told you that Bibi? She stared at me sadly like she was waiting for me to calm down. Abilena who told you that? But she wouldnt answer til I calmed down. I told her just keep fishing and dont worry your little head. Daddys taking care of everything. But I knew I was lying. When she started speaking again it was under her breth but I could hear every word. She said: if you take all the rusty coffee cans in the world and pour their coins out into a big pile we would be rich until the money died. And if you catch all the fish in the lake and pile them up til the sun. Then she stoped for a second. Well the top one would cook til the meat got tasty with garlic and butter. She said it just like that. Some sort of tiny poet. I didnt say anything. I wanted to cry. Maybe I did a little but I hid it from her and we continued fishing. Just the tears of a drunk. After a wile I told her no Bibi not in the reeds. Your gonna snag your line if you keep casting there. You need to find some nice open water near the dark spots.

When the suns out they escape to the shade. Thats where you gotta find them. She folowed the directions and cast her line with those thin arms. Always amazing those arms getting anything done at all. After some silence she started asking questions again. Why are his eyes red? Who? The fish. What fish? All of them in this lake. Well thats how he is Bibi. The peacock bass is angry cause god made him so beautiful and delicious. Then he made fishermen and their rods. I remember laughing and liting a cigarette. I caught one daddy she said. Im catching one. Steady Bibi steady now. Dont jerk the line too fast. Just reel him in slowly. Take it slow. If your arms get tired Im here to help you. Then I slammed its head upside the bow and let her hold it. The yellow white gills and bright red fin and the long green body painted black in careless stripes. Did all the trees burn? She asked me. No Bibi they just get dark to stay friends with the sun. Like you daddy? Just like me. One day Ill be as black and bald as the lake trees. Youl have children and Ill be a grandfather. I'm never gonna have kids daddy. I dont wanna get fat. I remember pearls trickling down my sides where my armpits were fairly raining sweat. But she kept cutting into me with her soft little questions. Do you love mom? What kind of a questions that Bibi? Well do you? Do I what? Love mom. Bibi Ive always stood by your mother I said. Thats what marriage means. It means to stand by no matter what even when things get hard. Why do things get hard daddy? Because lifes too long Bibi and after a while you cant help but notice. Thats when you find out what people are made of. Anybody can be good in the easy times but it takes a real man to get through the bad ones. So you love mom? Bibi pay attention to the fish. You should never kill anything absuntmindedly. Always know who your killing and why. Never eat the flesh of an animal unless youv thanked god for what hes given us. This lake would be empty without god and we would have no home or family. Always remember that Bibi. We're just visitors here. Did god make the lake trees Daddy? Every single one of them Bibi and he loves them all the same as I love you. I looked out over the bare water. The sun was shining so hot it looked like it had turned to gasoline. Listen to me Bibi because this is important. Theres nothing god isnt. Your perfect and Im perfect and Moms perfect. Thats why things matter so much Bibi. Cause their exactly as they are. For everybody? For everybody. What about the man with jelyfish eyes? Even for him Bibi. Maybe even more for him. But he cant see nothing. Sometimes thats a good thing. Sometimes our eyes make us blind. Now look the fish in the eyes Bibi. Dont let him die alone. FUCK Im crying now too. Gonna mess up this fucking notebook. Cant believe I was a man on earth and I told my doghter those things. Even if I failed her and Im a worthless old fuck living in the mountains alone nobody can take those times away from me.

School Dance (Age 17)

Pigeons sleep at night. All day they scrap for food, hopping the picnic tables and chewing old fries. Then the night spreads and *merengue* starts. Cause when the music quiets and the dancing pauses, then you can hear them crying their bird tears in the rafters. But Connie and I stand on the periphery of the big empty dance floor anyway, staring at the heels mom bought to help. She doesn't know about Nesto cause mom's too deluded to think I've already lost it.

They're not that bad, Abi.

They're pretty bad. Why would anybody wear these things? They're so uncomfortable.

Connie stares at my feet, then at my legs.

I fucking hate school dances. I'd set this building on fire but it's got no walls. It's like an open prison.

Connie has tits but wears sweaters so the boys don't look. She never uses makeup either. I don't think she even shaves her pits. If I wanna fuck I'll fuck, she told me once. I'm not a goddamn Barbie. I feel like an idiot standing next to her in my heels, the boys staring across the dance floor, their backs to the wall or standing around in circles drinking cokes and sprites. Some of them slip rum into the cans when the chaperone's not looking. Connie's arms are crossed under her tits and I can see her sharp teeth and scowling face. From the side she looks like someone else, but I'm not sure who. But I recognize Connie when she turns to me.

Fuck this place. There's no reason to be here.

Yeah, it's weird.

If you think about it, there's no reason to be anywhere. We stand a certain way, wear a certain thing, drink to feel better about ourselves and listen to this awful music. At best these monkeys will grind our thighs while we swing back and forth around the dancefloor. It's not even fun.

The *merengue* comes loud and grating from the pole-tip bullhorn speakers.

Es la vida, caja de sorpresas. Hoy felicidad o mañana tristeza. Hay dos caminos a escoger. Es lo que siempre ha brindado. Si escoges el equivocado. Adiós y que te vaya bien.

Abi, tonight you're gonna meet your true love. Your true, true love.

Shut up.

It's a fact. I can feel it in the air.

I hope you end up pregnant in *La Vega* but without me, just bloated and alone.

Connie's eyes shift blue and yellow and red. My legs like iron, smooth and gleaming under the cheap disco lights, toes mashed and propped uncomfortably. I close my eyes and think about this morning.

Aching when I finally rise to shit before he wakes, I flush quickly to avoid the smell and a second time after wiping. I'm glad Nesto isn't like the boys Connie sleeps with. He'd never try to lick my asshole. Maybe in the shower though? But I'm not like Connie and I slip quietly between the sheets, hoping he doesn't get up early and grog to the bathroom, half-hard and sniffing in horror. Brute. Ernesto. Helpless with long delicate eyelashes and shifting limbs. Chewing air and smacking his fat lips as he sleeps, unfazed by the noisy construction. They're hammering and scraping somewhere in the building. I asked Nesto about it the other day. What's that noise? It's the building settling, Bibi. It's nothing. Just go to sleep. But I know the truth about settling. It's just a pretty word for collapsing in slow motion. That's why we gotta hammer and scrape, cause everything would be flat and peaceful and we'd have nothing to our name.

Connie snaps her fingers in front of my face and I open my eyes. We look at the chipped metal benches to which we've carried so many steel-tray meals from the cafeteria. The earrings and braces and makeup of the rich Venezuelan girls turning to stare at *la rubia y la puta*. The Mormons less vicious but still unwilling to mix with our kind. Every day at this goddamn school and the nights too with disco lights but just the same, boring. And my body in stark immobility as the music insists, but I'm not in the mood. I'm never in the mood for these dances and I don't know what to do with myself. Connie's mouth is moving.

Why does your mom want you to come to these?

She still thinks I'm gonna find a boy to hold hands with. She wants me to be a normal girl.

You didn't tell her?

Are you crazy? She'd lose her mind. I can't tell mom anything, she'd completely fall apart.

What about your pops?

Dad doesn't remember shit. Ever since he started with morning rum it's real bad.

Sounds like mine. At least yours works. I think mine's a criminal.

You think? He sits around the pool all day and you never run out of money.

Ok, he's definitely a criminal. And my mom's an alcoholic.

My dad doesn't even catch the fish. He just answers his phone and makes sure the men take the tourists out on the lake. None of them speak English. They're all *morochos*.

Connie shrugs and stares at the dance floor.

I'm back with Nesto in the morning, his mouth open and snoring. Ernesto only sleeps late on the weekend, cause he's got a serious job with his Dad. He's no club rat.

We can't let him know, you realize, Abi. We can never tell Bill about this. He's already in a bad place.

What's wrong with Bill, Nesto?

I love him but he's always complaining. Things are never simple with him. It's hard to be around.

You mean at the sports club?

Yeah. But at the same time, I wanna help him. I just can't. I just can't do that stuff anymore.

What stuff?

The hanging round with nothing to do, drinking and getting older. *Tomando copas.* Talking shit and stumbling home at four AM. I want something for myself, Abi. I want a job and a family. I want to be normal.

So Bill's not normal?

Ernesto gets real quiet and I know the answer. Not cause he tells me, but cause I've known.

Let's stop talking about this, Abi. Let's talk about today. Today we can do anything you want. Let's go to

Caricuao. Let's go see your friends the parrots at the zoo. Let's go visit the sad hippos and drink fruit juices and eat *empanadas*. Let's go see the blind crocodile and hold hands.

Will you kill the *tigre* for me today?

Yes, I've been doing pushups, have you noticed?

How could I not. You're growing hair on your back like a gorilla. I've always wanted a real man. *Un macho de mierda.*

Let me be simple Abi, you know I don't understand things good.

Me speak good.

Me fuck good.

Let's see it then.

His awful breath gets better with time. Then it's too late to stop. We can't tell Bill. We can't tell.

I stand alone on the edge of the dance floor. Connie's with JC, swaying to a slow song, his face buried in her neck and fingers getting lower, the jackal. Won't ever forget the look on his face when he slapped Camilo's back and walked into the bathroom. I could see Connie through the crack in the door and she was drunk with her underwear around her ankles and smiling. Connie really shouldn't go near him anymore. She just likes making the other girls furious. I can't believe I told them what I saw. Guess JC would have told the boys anyway. Him and his crooked mouth. But Connie and I, we're friends now. I'll never betray her again. No matter what she does. But look at her. Even in jeans and a sweater she knows how to make the other girls angry.

Then the music stops and she dumps JC and we grab our backpacks and slip off into the night. It's cool behind the utility shed where we stifle our laughter and lean against the wall. Once everyone's gone and they lock the gates we leap down the concrete steps to the football field and unroll our sleeping bags next to each other.

Look at that clear sky.

Why didn't anyone ask me to dance, Connie?

I wouldn't worry about it. It's no big deal.

Still would've been nice if they'd asked.

They just think you're gonna say no, Abi.

Why would I say no?

You always say no. They just think you're frigid.

Well I'm not. I've got Ernesto.

Yes you do.

He's a good one.

I guess.

What do you mean, you guess?

Nothing. He's fine.

Then we're quiet and look up at the stars, feeling the early dew creep over us in quiet celebration. Connie makes a big deal of readjusting her sleeping bag and lays her head on my chest. I look down at her scalp, where the thick black hair touches the white skin. Much whiter than the rest of her. I put my hand on her forehead. It feels slightly moist. My hand begins to sweat. I wipe it against my sleeping bag. Connie lifts her head and rolls off onto her back again. We stay that way for a while.

You're a good friend, Connie.

No, you are.

I'm sorry about that thing.
I know you are. Stop saying you're sorry. It's boring and stupid.

Do you think Miss Mendoza's gonna come back?

I don't know. I hate her sub.

He's the worst. It's like having a second history class.

And he won't let me paint anything pink.

Maybe one day we should sneak in and paint the seat of his chair.

I'm sure his butt cheeks are pink enough. *Gringo de mierda.*

I'd have a handful of those raspberry buns.

He's ugly.

No, he's ugly and dumb, but I'd still fuck him. Then he'd get fired!

You're the worst.

I'm the best there ever was. See those stars in the middle? See how they're shaped like my face?

No.

Then you haven't looked hard enough.

Ok, I'll try.

You can write a book about me, Abi, I'm unforgettable.

You're like a yeast infection.

The best kind.

Do you ever smell weird after you bleed?

Always.

Do you think boys notice?

I hope not. They probably just think a fish truck's passing. Just don't let them go down there. Make them poke you in the fishcake with their harpoon.

You're a princess.

You're a nun.

Did you see what happened to Miss O'Sullivan today?

No.

She got hit in the head by a pigeon.

You're kidding.

Nope. She was walking down the path from the cafeteria, wearing those red heels and trying to look dignified, and then smack, a dirty pigeon flew right into her head. It was better than christmas.

Christmas sucks anyway.

I know.

What did she say?

She didn't say shit. Just kept walking and pretending it didn't happen. But everybody was laughing cause we all saw what happened.

How many of you?

Watching?

Yeah.

The whole biology class. We were waiting for Mister Calderon to set up an outdoor experiment. I think that pigeon was just horny. He wanted to fuck that beautiful perm.

So do you.

Yeah, I'd rub her big perm with my sloppy cunt.

Gross.

Radical.

Should we sleep?

Maybe.

Let's try.

Ok.

Sleep well, Abi.

You too Cons. I hope a pigeon doesn't shit in your mouth.

I stay awake for a few moments, waiting to see if Connie will put her head back on my chest. Then I fall asleep with the *merengue* still playing in my mind.

Hoy felicidad o mañana tristeza. Si escoges el equivocado. Adiós y que te vaya bien.

The Rainy Season (Age 17)

She falls in heavy, whipping rushes, flooding the sewers, popping manholes, and running the gutters. All day the smell of almost-rain as the sky swells low, heavier and heavier til the birds cry out and the clouds burst. Then the rain splits to mist and drifts through the rusty window bars. Pregnant. So I'm forming a dew, mossy and pulled open on the bed, trying to remember how this happened. Ok so he pulled me, no I pulled him. Then we'll definitely use them, he said, I'd like to be safe. But we didn't. And deep inside, in the place that isn't a place, I can feel the beginning of something. Are your nipples. You ripped the posters, Abi, why you ripped them. Goodbye teenager. Goodbye posters. Hello mama. I'm coming home she's coming home they're coming home. I'm so hungry I could eat a whole loaf of bread from the pantry with margarine and sugar and *maizena*. Are you swollen like the tadpoles in the still, warm water? Remember the day dad hooked Bill right past the barb, up to the shank? I could see his naked white butt. Dad couldn't pull it out. You caught Bill! Dad fished Bill. They had to cut him open to pull out the hook. He yelled. Are your nipples swollen? I pull my shirt up. It feels so good when we don't use them, he said. We should be safe, Abi. I wanna feel you pushing the walls, but I don't say that. Now look where it got you. I hold my breasts, my big swollen breasts. When my fingers touch the swollen parts it's the same as when I'm on my period but without all the blood. I feel so damn light. I can see that everything's gonna be alright. It's not a landscape cause there's no land. It's not a place cause it's no place. It's just where everything starts, and it's full. The mosquitoes do it and the fish do it and the flamingos do it and we do it. Everything's gonna be just fine. I wrestled him to the log and already knew it. I gotta tell Nesto I'm pregnant. Mom can't know. Dad can't know. Bill's not around to know. I'll go buy the test tomorrow but there's no need. For now I'm just lying here in the light spray, letting the water drum pretty without his smooth brown body and crooked smile.

Sarah — April 2nd, 1996

I often miss Abilena. She was a nurturing spirit. I realize now, with some distance, that I was simply ill-equipped to understand a child of her temperament. My strict upbringing, no matter how unsuitable, was all I knew how to pass on. This morning, as I was praying, I recalled the golden afternoon she returned home from school with an avocado pit. She had followed the teacher's instructions and suspended it with toothpicks in a glass of water. Abilena had always loved to watch things grow, and during that period she rose every morning before breakfast to wander down into the garden and inspect the pit. Soon the roots came, winding irreversibly through the virgin water, and her eyes lit up with childish pride. It was like Christmas morning for her.

In the following weeks Abilena watched over the plant as if it were her child. Once the roots had begun curling around the bottom of the glass, she ceremoniously marched into the garden and planted it into the hard brown soil. I provided her a small shovel, but she insisted on doing it with her bare hands instead. "To make the bed for the baby." She returned to the house with chipped nails and bleeding fingers, and that night I scolded her severely but was unable to dampen her high spirits.

Some time later, to my surprise, the plant began growing at a stupendous rate. Every day Abi sat and spoke to the tree, making sure to water the roots until its branches grew long and sturdy, just as she grew into her own awkward adolescent body. In her fits of teenage brooding she would often climb the avocado tree and disappear into its generous green foliage. She missed many a meal in this fashion, surviving simply on the fruit it bore her. Driven mad by her behavior, I berated her relentlessly for it, and now cannot help but look back on these nagging lectures with a sense of regret. If only I'd been a softer, more forgiving mother, then perhaps... but what is the point of these morbid reflections? Are they not the auto-flagellations of a self-appointed martyr? God rid me of such grandiosity.

AFFIRMATIONS:
I am grateful for what God gave me.
My daughter is in His hands.
~~The past is not real. How could it be?~~
~~No chocolate for me.~~

No family for me. A-F is criticizing me for my supposedly inexpert folding of the bed sheets, the cow. But it isn't just her. All the sisters are disappointed with me. "Have you been tearing out pages, Sarah? Have you been hiding things from us? God sees everything." Well let me inform you, sisters, that everyone's expectations are putting quite the strain on me. I'm dealing with psychological issues that none of you would understand.

Let me tell you what I enjoy, what gives me peace: the taste of crumpled paper and ink. I find peace in chewing. In fact I think I'll continue to swallow these pages rather than deal with your judgment. Even you, Claudia. I know you look down on me. The tone of your advice has shifted. You now speak to me as if I'm a spoiled child. Well I suppose I deserve it. To be an object of pity among the pitiful.

The lord sees everything? What would He say if He spoke to me? "Sarah, I want you to suffer greatly. This your cross to carry. Keep folding the sheets. Here, please accept my gift of A-F, whose role will be to pester you from dawn until dusk. Your ancestors have committed great and unforgivable sins."

Father was a Hitler Youth, or so I gleaned from dinner jokes. No wonder I married a barbarian. Mother did the same. But after the war there were no Nazis. Only opportunities abroad. Mother suggested England. Father suggested Venezuela. "I have some friends there. *Keine probleme*. You will enjoy the sunlight" I was eight years old. He told me, "Sarah, perhaps it's best you identify with your mother's side of the family from now on." (I was too embarrassed to look at him, but do remember his voice quivering weakly, and recall feeling deeply disappointed in the man.) It was the first time I saw him display any form of emotion. Losing the war meant a great deal to my father. He was even forced to affect a British accent, change his entire wardrobe, and make new friends (after remaining virtually friendless for a long period). We kept our money but he lost his country, and with it died his pride and the disciplinarian within him. He became loose and shabby, and a defeated atmosphere hung about him like a cheap veil.

Although we had no drawing room in the Venezuelan ranch house (oh I remember our house in Stuttgart was so beautiful, never too warm nor too cold, not a fly in sight, hand-carved balustrades leading to the top floor), father continued to teach me history in the afternoons, chair pulled up to the small table in the dining room. I remember the smell of fermented hops on his breath as he taught me about the British Empire and the Queen's Manners. (Never again did he mention the Treaty of Versailles or the Third Reich, both central to his previous lessons.) I would sit on his knee and sweat in the tropical heat (we had only a small electric fan in those days, no air conditioning) until the Kings and Queens became mixed up in my head. The tropics have a way of turning one's brains into a swirling mud pit; it's a miracle anybody living south of the equator learns anything, really.

Although these later lessons marked the beginning of father's physical affection for me (in Stuttgart I would sit on a separate chair beside him, and he never drank beer) I don't remember them fondly. He held me too tightly, touched me too pathetically, and would not cease repeating himself until he became like a broken record. "Never speak of Stuttgart, Sarah. Never speak of Germany. What is the current King's name?" "George VI, father." "The prince?" "There is no prince, father." "The princess?" "There are two. Elizabeth and Margaret." Soon I was desperate to memorise the whole family tree, that I might never again be forced to sit on his warm knee, both feet hanging above the ground, his thick fingers wrapped around my midriff. I quickly learned the Queen's Manners by heart.

Keine probleme, Claudia, I'll tell the sisters everything.

I'll tell them things even God doesn't want to remember. After all, the sun never sets on the British Empire, and I can see every dazzling bit of it. In fact it's burning my eyes out.

The Root Canal (Age 17)

I'm invisible from the third branch up, hidden by leaves and unripe avocados, green and smooth and swaying from the climb. I feel hot all over too, like so many lamps in the hothouse, where the wet heat stays young forever cause of the butterflies. Plus I'm climbing this tree pregnant, hoping the baby won't fall out of me, cause from this high up, well

It's so beautiful inside here, so green.

Inside the avocado lives a pit. Inside the pit lives a yellow muck. Inside the yellow muck lives the beginning of another avocado tree.

I pick one from the branch and tear it open. The flesh is blackened and ancient but I don't even care, I'd eat anything, the blacker the better the deader the butter. Anything. Then I feel my tooth split like ice under a hammer, and suddenly I remember Bill. Of course! It's one of his BB pellets. He left the metal seed in the ripe avocado, and it stayed in the muck to remind me of his self, but now it's too late, I already ate the memory of Bill, and it tasted like the dry flesh of a mummified child. No, no, I can still see the way he used to squint when he leaned on the balcony and aimed his rifle at the avocadoes.

Yes of course! It's from the time I was in the tree and Billy started shooting like a madman, and I froze in silence and waited, pellets tearing through the leaves like an angry swarm of silver bugs. I even saw him hit the avocado, the one I just ate, cause at the time it protected me from his violence, and the pellet was heading straight for my eyeball. Bill would never do things so directly. That's not how he works. Instead he left the pellet inside the avocado, where it waited patiently for the opportunity to smash my tooth open and reveal a red mulch, raw and filled with hurt. I look at the pellet in my open palm, rolling it around in the fresh blood.

So this is how Bill's violence exists. It lives in the germ of all things, swelling like feed in the breast, like an avocado that stays on the tree and turns black without falling, or a flamingo that never grows wings. Like trees born bare from the wasted waters, or shrimp born blind in the mud. And that's why I cannot keep it. I cannot

Cannot what, Abi?

I just can't.

Nesto pulls me in.

I don't really know what you're talking about. Are you alright?

Yeah.

Have you been smoking pot?

You know I don't smoke pot.

I know, but you've been floating around for days. You're happier than I've ever seen you.

I'm just happy, Nesto.

I sit up, feeling him grow. I unbutton my blouse and unhook my bra. Nesto's eyes are sad and brown.

You're just so beautiful, Abi.

Put them in your mouth.

I hold the back of his head. The mosquito draws blood from his shoulder, its belly swelling red.

Use your teeth.

The mosquito pulls its needle from his skin.

Harder. Bite me harder, Nesto. Oh, Nesto.

I use my hands to guide it. So the walls know, and the ache is without pain. Just the knowledge is enough to make me come, pressing my palm to his chest to make sure he doesn't move.

Abi, I love you.

Nesto, I need you to fill me up til my belly's red and tight.

Abi, are you listening to me? I love you.

Don't say that, Nesto.

His eyes are closed.

It's true, Abi, I can't help it.

After I climb down from the tree I hold the gauze to my cracked tooth and mom drives me to the hospital. The doctor has a small black moustache and speaks very quickly.

It's not called mulch, young lady. It's actually a pulp. What we're going to do is remove that pulp. Your tooth will be fine, because it's being fed by the blood in your gums. We're going to give you local anesthesia, so you shouldn't feel much. Then we'll fill it up and you'll be on your way. Is everything alright?

But if you put me to sleep, you'll kill it.

No, your tooth should be fine. There's no need to worry.

I don't know if I want to kill it.

Abilena, your tooth won't fall out.

Mom, you don't understand.

Abi, what are you going on about? Mr. Selvez is a professional orthodontist. You'll be fine.

He'll kill the baby!

What baby?

My baby.

Abi, what are you talking about? Are you pregnant?

Yes.

Mom's watching a television show about me. Her eyes are blank. Mr. Selvez performs the root canal successfully and cements the tooth. Mom drives me home in silence. Just the sound of cars til I realize I'm drooling all over my tank top. Really can't feel much.

Nesto's still inside me, spent eyes closed in prayer.

I'm ready to tell you.

Tell me what?

I'm pregnant.

I can see it born in his eyes, like a drop of blood in a glass of water. He'll never be simple again. The idea's now inside him like the baby's inside me.

Before browny died, and browny's definitely dead, I watched her stand in front of the mirror, staring at her own reflection. From each of her eyes came a black snail-trail, but she wasn't weeping from shame. No way. Browny was just a woman with nobody to watch her, not even herself. That's why we tie the dog to a post. We're scared of her freedom. Cause when browny looked in the mirror, all she saw was the sound of the wind in the avocado leaves. But we're more complicated, us. Even Nesto.

So I watch him stare at my belly, then bring his eyes up to mine. He shifts slightly across the bed, putting some space between us, cause when you dance you need somewhere to put your feet, and Nesto wants very badly to dance with me.

Abi, let's have the baby. I'm ready. You know I'm ready. I've got the job. I can support us. We could be a family.

I look at the swollen tip of his prick, where the trickle's congealing. Nesto naked, one leg bent, spine to the wall, eyebrows thick and black and stupid.

You know I love you, Abi.

You tell me often enough.

Don't be cruel.

If a wasp dies, it doesn't have any power left. The ants carry it away like a blade of grass. But Nesto has a heart. And Nesto has big useless arms. Cause mom had me. Dad made me into mom and mom made me into the world. So if I were a mother I'd buy a chair and watch the betamaxes come crashing down. One day the ants would carry me away in my sleep, like a sleeping bag in the shape of a woman. No I cannot be a mother. I cannot keep it.

I'm not sure, Nesto.

Then why can't you let me be sure for the both of us? I'll take care of us, I swear it. *Te lo juro.*

I have to think about it, Nesto. I'm seventeen.

Don't you feel good today?

Yes, I feel perfect. I've never felt better. But maybe it's not my baby.

Abi, what the fuck are you talking about?

Maybe it's just a baby.

Are you telling me I'm not the father?

You're a father. Maybe it's your baby.

My baby? But it's your womb. You and I made it together.

But sometimes the flamingo has a broken leg and the red heron takes care of it.

Abi, I don't know what the fuck's gotten into you, but you're not making any sense.

Sorry. Maybe we should talk about this some other time.

No. This time you're not gonna stay silent. You never fucking answer me. It's always your way. Nobody's cut your tongue, and I have a right to know what's happening.

I don't know what's happening, I don't have any answers.

That's not good enough. You're happy. You're pregnant. Isn't that simple? Can't it be simple for once?

I'm sorry.

I can't fucking believe it. You need help, Abi. You're losing your mind.

Maybe, but I'm not gonna lose my body.

Nesto stands rigid, facing away from the bed. His whole body trembles. There's a place where things happen, but they always happen too fast. Then you see them from the bed, as he walks into the bathroom, each step slow and painful. And when you stand under the waterfall, you can't hear yourself scream. Cause the water's so white there's no sound at all. So Nesto's smashing the bathroom to bits, but I can't even hear it from the bed, cause I'm at the center, where the mist floats and you can't hear nothing but water beating water. Of course I don't know. Nobody knows. I whisper it. Nesto screams it. But the animals don't need to say a goddamn thing.

Daniel — 15 of August of 1997

WHAT REALLY HAPPENED ON VIERNES NEGRO!!!

On the 18th of February 1983 the bolivar lost half its worth overnight. The motherfuckers in the *Herrera Campins* administraton tipped off the RICH GRINGOS and VENEZUELAN ARISTOCRATS who made a killing buying dollars before the fall. They stole most of the countrys money while everybody was asleep. From that day on we lived in the busted dream of the Venezuelan middle class. My debt was a timebomb and I stopped opening mail from the bank. I couldnt do a damn thing about it anyway. THEY KNEW WHAT THEY WERE DOING. IT WAS A FUCKING INSIDE JOB. The oil boom was over and Iran was exporting again. SO THEY SAW IT COMING AND THEY PLANNED IT. Anybody who believed in the bolivar got royally screwed. THEY SCREWED THE WORKING CLASS. THEY SUNK MY FAMILY. THE CORUPT GOVERMENT AND THE GRINGOS WORKING WITH THE CIA. Inflacion hasnt stopped since. Newspapers started printing the exchange rate on the front page every day on account of it falling so fast. Just thinking about that day makes me madder than hell. Even Sarah noticed things get shittier. I never spoke to her about the debt but she knew. Every motherfucker knew. The party was over.

Mom's Decision (Age 17)

I never heard him swear like he swore on black friday. They called it *viernes negro* cause dad's money died and his voice rose shaking from the walls to make the house angry.

Herrera, you son of a bitch. *Hijo de puta de mierda.* How much did they pay you? Your mother's a whore of the lowest kind. I spit on your grave and your children's graves. Get fucked in hell where you deserve to burn *para toda la eternidad.*

So nobody went to school that day. All the kids in Caracas sat in their bedrooms with the doors locked. I lay on my bed listening to dad smash glasses as he screamed about the president bending over for the *gringos.*

When there were no more glasses and no more plates, silence fell over the house. Still the dogs howled across the valley, and still I listened to them. But mom would never see England again, cause nobody wanted our money. There was something rotten living inside our country, and nobody knew about it yet. It was like the red sickness in dad's radio, and nobody found out til we cracked it open and looked inside. Sometimes avocados are like that, spidered with darkness and tasting of rot. It happens in the places we never look.

Finally I open my door and tiptoe up the stairs. There's broken glass on the kitchen floor and all the mirrors are broken. Dad's sitting on the sofa but I can tell he's too sweet to be awake. His hand's hanging over the armrest, palm open, dripping blood in a pool of yellow light. I hate that goddamn lamp, making his rum shine with its cheap shade. Dad's knuckles are glassy and torn, hanging limp above the marble floor. You're so goddamn sweet. Are you done yelling? Is there anything else you'd like to break? Don't you hear the dogs crying in the valley? Don't you know you're not alone? I button his shirt and take the bottle from his fingers. I walk to the balcony and pour out the rum. It takes a second before I hear it hitting the grass. I use all my strength and the bottle clears the fence. Then I repeat the same thing with all the other bottles of rum in the pantry. One by one I hear them smash on the asphalt. The last bottle hits the fence and bounces back into the yard. There's a dark puddle on the grass below the balcony. Still he doesn't wake up. So I walk back inside and sit next to dad on the sofa. Then I remember the blood.

When I walk through their bedroom, mom calls out to me through the darkness.

Abi.

Yes, mom.

What are you doing?

Don't worry about it.

I do. I do worry about it. You're my baby. You'll always be my baby.

Yes, mom.

In the bathroom I find gauze and mercurochrome and cotton balls.

Oh Abi, Abi, Abi.

Sleep, mom. Just sleep.

I walk back up the stairs and he hasn't moved. I pull the glass bits from dad's knuckles by lamplight. There's more and more blood, and I soak it up with the extra gauze, but every time I sponge it, there's more pooling in the little holes. Dad's hand is a spit. It's built on the blood. But glass still grows there, cause dad's a stubborn son of a bitch. After most of the gauze is gone, the blood slows down a bit. I soak a cotton ball in mercurochrome and apply it to the holes. Red on red. Can't tell the blood from the medicine. Can't tell the rum from the water. Can't tell Bill what we're doing. Then I apply three cotton balls to the knuckles and wrap the hand in gauze. I place his hand on his lap and pull his other arm over my shoulder. With my head pressed to his chest, I can hear his heart beating water. Jesus turned water into wine. Dad turned water into rum and rum into blood. Then the red heron came and turned blood into water again. And we were fishing on the lake when dad spoke. I promise I'll never leave you, he said. I promise you, Bibi. I know I'm not a perfect father, but I promise you we'll get old together.

His bottom lip's sloping down and he's drooling on his shirt. I hold it up but it won't stay. Dad's heavy but I work him upright and his head tilts back a little.

I'll take care of you til the day you die. Cause I love you, dad.

When the sun comes up, the dogs are quiet and the valley's covered in fog. I creep down into the garden and toss the last bottle over the fence, watching it smash to bits in the street. Still a circle of brown grass where I poured the rum last night.

Brush my teeth and get dressed and catch the school bus with an empty stomach. No matter, I'll get a banana from the stand. He always gives me one. He likes me. From the bus window I can see plenty of people passed out, their bodies propped against the graffiti. *LA MIERDA*. Others wander through the street, stumbling drunk and tripping on curbs. Most have worn knees and no shoes. The smashed glass of looted stores. Cardboard boxes and plastic wrapping and shopping carts with missing wheels. Caracas is a garbage heap.

The old man has jellyfish eyes, and I watch him from the stoplight as he sticks a crude finger into one nostril and blows a slug out the other. Then the right side. He's smiling like crazy.

At school the hallways are mostly empty. There's lots of lost *bolivares*, I guess. Lots of smashed glasses. Can't really concentrate in class, but it doesn't matter cause they're just showing movies. I'm a fucking adult anyway. Almost done with all this shit. At lunch I sit with Connie against the lockers and Miss Mendoza walks by.

Miss!

Girls!

She's so beautiful with her shaved head, bright blue eyes, and long green dress. Miss Mendoza's body is a real body, to travel and climb with, to run and love with, to fight and paint with. I hold it close.

How've you two been?

Shit since you left Miss. Your sub's a real pencil dick.

I've been painting a lot!

More pink, Abi?

Not just, Miss, I've also been painting on wooden boards I find in the street.

I'd love to see some of it. I'm curating an exhibition soon, and it's gonna be pretty diverse. I'd love to show some bleeding-heart teenage art. Your heart's still bleeding right?

Every day, Miss, every single day.

Well here's my number, make sure you call me.

I promise to paint this card pink and never call you.

Good girl.

So you're a curator now?

I guess so. Mostly I've been baking cunt cookies and selling them at art expos and fairs.

You're a hero, Miss.

Thanks Connie. I do what I can. I've been making prick cookies too, just so they don't feel left out.

Beasts.

Simpletons.

Macacos.

Handsomes.

Cowboys.

God, it's so good to see you.

Well now that I'm not a teacher anymore, we can see more of each other.

Now we're just a cunt gang trying to take over the world.

You haven't changed, Connie.

You neither, Miss.

I'm gonna go make sure pencil dick's still teaching you how to make art.

Oh please, Miss. He's a fucking historian.

History's important too, girls. Today of all days you should remember that. But it doesn't always have to be written by fat old white men.

The slobs.

I'll see you two around the bend. *Hasta luego, lindas.*

Bye Miss!

And then the day's good, cause we're all in this together and I know what to do. Plenty's gonna happen, and I'll be there for all of it. Cause the country's gone to shit but there's everything to live for. I'm alive on this earth as an artist and we sit together, staining our skirts on the bright green grass.

Cons, you're a great friend.

No, you are Abi.

I keep looking down, cause Connie's staring at me.

And the sun's hot as ever when she leans in to kiss me on the mouth.

Did you like it?

Yes, um. Yes. It was nice.

Cause I really like you, Abi.

I like you too.

But in her eyes I can see how she means it. Many things I can't abandon and every body deserves a prayer. Dad's and Mom's and Billy's and Nesto's and Connie's. There's beauty everywhere and I want to be on my knees washing it all with soap like Jesus and the feet. Connie smiles at me.

If you want I can kiss you down there.

Connie!

I'm tingling but I turn away and Connie lies on her back and I do the same. We look up at the sky and see the things we're thinking about. I see Miss Mendoza and the art show and the cunt cookies and the way her shaved head looks strong and sleek. It's all up there in the cloudless blue. In fact there's nothing black about the sky today.

When I get home, dad's gone. Out with the fishermen, mom tells me, and stares at the television. I kiss her forehead and she doesn't seem to notice.

She's left something for me on my bedside table. It's a white box with no label and a little post-it note.

Put four deep inside you. Six hours later, put four more. There are pads in the bathroom. You will probably need them. Make sure have someone there with you when you do this, darling. It may hurt. PS: Please flush this note down the toilet so your father does not find it. He would not understand.

I crumple the note into a ball and toss it in the garbage can. Lie on my bed in my school clothes, and that's how I wake up the next morning. But the box is still there.

Sarah — April 11th 1996

<u>AFFIRMATIONS</u>
Today is a new day, and a new opportunity to be cleansed of my past.
No sin is too great to be forgiven.
Peace is available at any moment.
The sisters are here to guide me.

I told Claudia what I did to my grandchild and wept in her arms. I had never spoken about it to a single soul. How foolish of me, in retrospect, to think I could hide it from God. I expected her to chastise me, but she remained very calm and told me I had been forgiven a long time ago. "Your challenge now, Sarah, is to find compassion for yourself." Claudia is a saint. Nonetheless I killed that child. I can beg forgiveness but it won't change the facts.

Unless God wanted it dead and I was doing His work, preventing our family's rotten genes from being passed on to a new generation. Would the child, if it had been carried to term, been born with the same mark as William? Doomed to repeat the same patterns?

~~"You never mention your son, Sarah. Why is that?" Because, Claudia, what kind of god would take my first born son, my baby~~

God, please forgive me. You will find me in prayer, looking inwards and waiting for a sign.

Spit in the Mask (Age 17)

It's chewing my guts by the time I reach his door.

Pequeña, what the fuck are you doing here?

Oh, Bill.

When the coral's gone, the reef gets eaten by the salt water til the holes come. Cause all the fish and the anemones are gone, so nobody's home to stand guard. Then the settling starts, til nothing's left but the ocean floor, and nobody's there to tell the story, even in gurgles.

Bill's face has settled plenty, and there's new shade under his cheeks. His eyes are red and his hair's thin, and Bill's got nothing but salt water flowing through him. It always eats everything and leaves the red sickness. Like Bill's ruined apartment. The smell of old curry and vinegar, sharp as fishbone and burning my nostrils. Already he's got me wrapped in his white arms speckled with rust. Still able to carry me to the ratty sofa and put a pillow under my head.

Little one, what's happening to you? Are you coming down? You're sweating like crazy.

I put four of them in my cunt, like mom said.

What are you talking about?

I didn't know, Bill. I didn't know who to call. Couldn't tell Connie. Couldn't tell. Ah. Couldn't tell him.

Who? Couldn't call who? Who's him?

Couldn't call you, cause your phone always rings busy. So I just came over. It hurts, Bill. It hurts.

How did you get here?

I took the. Ah. The fucking bus.

Are you out of your mind? You can't just wander into the *barrio*. You're a fucking girl.

I didn't have a choice. And if it's so bad. If the *barrio* is so bad. Why do you live in it?

Abi. You don't get it. Things are fucked here. Two weeks ago they cleaned out my apartment. They took my phone, my television. Thank god they left the light bulbs. They came over with black ski masks and AK-47s. I gotta get the fuck out of here, Abi. It's not safe. You shouldn't have come.

Everyone seemed plenty nice on my way over. I asked them how to find your apartment and they all. Ah. They called you. That nickname. *Rojo flaco*. I said yeah, skinny red's my brother. And they showed me where to go. Ah. It really fucking hurts.

What did you take, Abi?

I'm pregnant, but the pills are taking care of it. It's like. It's like a fire down there, I'm burning up. I think something's wrong. It's like a hot piece of metal sawing through my guts.

They didn't give you anything for the pain? You can't just suffer like an idiot. I'm gonna give you something.

Ok, Bill.

So he disappears into the bathroom. The walls are fading pink and spidered with cracks. There's plenty stains too, and torn surfers. A coffee table covered with styrofoam and food and flies and cigarette butts and plastic cups, tearing and clawing at each other in the whistling bonfire. The floor of the *barrio* takes all my blood. The floor of the world is bloody towels and stained carpeting and fish heads and wilted lettuce and children drinking from puddles and women hanging their laundry on the cement grid and the corrugated metal of endless poverty stacked to the sky and screaming about football through sliced coca cola bottles. They pull electricity from shack to shack across the dirt roads and they smoke cigarettes and eat fried *yuca* and smile and yell and drink and fight and fuck and burn cigarette holes in my belly. The ground is shifting lava, thank you very much. The ground is a living volcano of torn guts spitting hot pain through my stomach and out my cunt. And the tile floors are smeared with blackened paste, endlessly bleeding til I soak pad after white pad. Thank god I brought them. And Bill's pills. They better help.

Don't worry. Don't worry. You're gonna be fine.

And the wet rag's cold on my forehead as Bill sits over me.

It's not our baby. It's not my time.

I know, *pequeña*, don't sweat it. I'm gonna take care of you.

She left the box just like that. Didn't say nothing. Ah. Nobody's gonna get in there, it's gonna be me and the pills. Nobody. But why'd you stop coming to the beach?

I'm swimming downstream on my belly, but the stream's too shallow and the rocks beat my knees and thighs and belly and breasts and arms and face. Long strips of torn flesh, caught on the rocks and flapping in the stream. *Y los pirañas.* From the sides. But there's no relief. I'm moving too fast to stop. Like the slide how it torn that kid.

Like the summer you stepped on a wasp, Bill. Everyone could hear you crying for half an hour. Mom kissed your foot and Dad told you to be a man.

Fuck dad. And try to shut up, *pequeña*. You need to rest. Soon it'll kick in. You're feverish.

But he just pushes me downstream more and more, til the bottom parts're gone and I'm pulping on the rocks as the *piraña* fish, scraping and scraping in the infected waters. Then the river widens and the delta's under me, free of rocks and pebbles and stones and sand. Nothing's solid in the delta, and soon the open ocean heals my wounds and carries me in its wet arms.

You're gonna be fine. The codeine's working. It'll take the pain away.

But I know the fire's burning, just a room away, where the velvet delta spurts red from the sharp rocks to make it all come out. Make it all come out. Empty me of this life you've chosen. Blank like Bill like blanket like Bill. Go on. Don't stop now. So I stand up and change the pad again. Floating plenty cause Bill's here with his rotten dishes and yellow teeth and pale green eyes.

You're so beautiful, Bill.

Shush.

But it's not our baby. Cause you left us. Cause *rojo flaco* is what they call you now. Oh Bill. Thanks for taking care of me.

Shush now. Stay quiet.

So the bubbles rise to the surface of his face. Real Bill says spit in the mask, *pequeña*, that way it doesn't get all fogged up. Then you rub it in with your finger. *Entiendes?* Yeah I get it. Let's go see the fish. Ok. But don't go too far, make sure you stay real close to me. Promise?

I promise. Good. Then let's go. With the flippers you can push through the water much faster, even though it burns your legs when you do it. But the fish don't care if you're there. They don't even run when you stare at them close. They wear black stains over their eyes with silver and blue stripes. Look, Bill! He gives me the OK sign, cause the thumbs up means let's go back. So you should never use the thumbs up. OK. The fish are so pretty. And all the little beasts are opening and closing. But too far down there's also the eels and once I saw a barracuda. Don't worry none, unless there's blood. Cause if there's blood, and he makes the face, then they're gonna come and eat you up! And he tickles me til I scream and run and kick and cry. Stop it, Bill! Stop it.

Pequeña, wake up. You're dreaming. Calm down.

How many. How many hours has it been, Bill? Since I came over.

About three.

Then I have to do something.

Can I help you?

No, it's just me. It's just me.

I stand up and get dizzy and sit down a little. Then I go to the bathroom and take the four pills out of my pocket and pull down my undies to check. The blood's a thick paste. I wipe what I can and push the pills as far as possible, up into the walls, making sure there's no doubt about it. Don't feel bad. It's not time. It's not mine. I'm gonna be an artist. I'll paint you onto a canvas someday, I promise you. I think of you, don't worry. The fourth pill's done. So that's it. I replace the pad and wash my face in the broken mirror. Not shattered by a fist, but shattered by time. And only one of the light bulbs work. They came with ski masks. Jesus christ, Bill. So I stay on the couch, getting ready as Bill hands me the watermelon juice.

Drink it.

I chew the rice and try my best. Bill is tapping his foot on the floor. Tap, tap, tap.

You're gonna be fine. You know I love you, right?

I know, Bill. Thanks for doing this.

You're welcome. I'm glad I'm here to help. I know I haven't been round.

No you haven't.

I know. But things are different for me. You're a girl. And things with dad. You know. And mom. I mean. It's all fucked up and I can't do anything. I had to leave.

Uhuh.

But I think of you all the time.

Why don't you come to the sports club anymore?

Cause I've got no friends there. Everyone's gone. They all have boring jobs and kids now. It's fucking depressing.

Ok.

But I'll make an effort, Abi. I'll try to be around more often. I always like to see you. You know that.

I know that.

So I quiet down and try to get ready. But nothing prepares me for the pain. So minuscule and precise, like grains of sand burning their way through my guts and out my back. The jolting rain that burns through everything with its plick, plock, plick.

Bill. Help me. For the love of god, give me the pills again. Take it away, Bill. Take it away.

I've got none left, Abi.

Find something! *Hijo de puta*!

Abi. I only have grass.

Then give me some grass!

Ok. Calm down. Fucking relax.

But the screams don't stop. I suck on the little glass

pipe and cough til it hurts. So it fills me, that slow warm calm. The rain falls but the pillow makes holes so the mosquitoes can get through without touching the netting. But I'm falling asleep like a stupid idiot. Cause I can see the blood on the canvas and it's perfect. Just find a pillow to make into a person and let it bunch in the corner til everything's fine. Yeah the room must be closed then. Cause the walls are like star wars in the *barrio*.

Don't let it pull me under.

Shush.

But the black edges are just lines of ants. Every angle has ants. And Bill's face is smudged like the inside of a car. Nothing's clean in this room forever. You can never go back.

Bill, things are very bad.

They're fine.

No they're not. Something's wrong. What did I smoke, Bill? It tastes weird.

Oh, fuck.

What?

The grass. I mean. I think there was some DMT left in the pipe.

What's DMT?

It's um. It only lasts half an hour.

But it's forever now. Cause everything's crumbling and there's only oil, the thick black sludge of everything sinking and sinking. Now listen to me, Abi. The brother's talking to the sister cause I can see them in the walls where the flies eat old chinese food. Slippery little worms. You're gonna trip for half an hour, but remember it's just a drug. Don't let the knives come crawling from the open red strawberries if you can't see where they are. I'm me. But she's. Not a face, sinking into the tickling grass when you can't feel nothing. And the heart ain't gonna keep going neither. Dying right here before I show the paintings to Miss Mendoza. Cause Connie loves me and I need to save Mommy and Daddy. Those people aren't my Abilena. I'm Abilena. I'm Abilena. But it doesn't mean my body's a body. In the end, there's a smaller one inside the big one if you wanna open your eyes. There's a perfect dot, and within that dot, there's infinite amounts of everything you can see, all the time. Cause every detail never ends unless you cut into the sludge with a knife and say, right here. Here's where it stops. Where it stop? Not in the beginning, cause you came from this. And not in the end, cause you're not. She's gonna die cause she's dead. Heart stopped cold as a rock in her chest, weighing into the pillow and too thick to go through. It died, it died. None of the books and the movies and the songs and the clothes and the skin and the eyes and the face and the years and the mom and the dad and the none, none, none, none. Shoot into the sky and explode like a firework, from the cold center of the heart and into the universe, where all dead things rest forever, sending light long-since extinguished to be reflected by bloody rum and glass knuckles. Thirty minutes. Oh but it'll be thirty minutes til thirty minutes. Cause in five minutes time'll stop, cause it's not happening when it needs to. We're late again in thirty minutes. Nothing's catching. Broken bits of glass are pouring from the delta and into the ocean, torn to shreds by the barracuda's face, white and sculpted in salt. And sometimes things are born of the diamond dark, chiseled into dust and pushed into the sea. So nothing can't be naked in the world of things, no matter how close. You're gonna be fine. But why's it so scary? Cause you're told too fast when you're told, and you're never told if you're not. So half of them go crazy, and the other half live dully in the shadow of god. So nothing's gonna be, cause everything already was. But still the room's cut from shadow and light, and placed on earth. And Bill sits next to the bed, looking at me with his big green eyes, cause he don't know. So when my fingers touch his face as he holds them tight, there's a moment where the water hangs caught between two lashes before it runs long, past the nose and onto the edge of his mouth.

Sarah — April 14th, 1996

AFFIRMATIONS
~~Blame serves nobody.~~
~~Blame is not God's will for me.~~

Oh how those words sound like Daniel's! "Blame never helped nobody". That's what he once said, the imbecile. He was speaking about me, of course. I was the one who needed to stop blaming him. "Some of these American tourists, honey. They like to hug to say hello and goodbye." But it wasn't the smell of perfume that bothered me. It was the nauseating undercurrent of sweat, vaginal secretions, urine, and (tying this noxious bouquet together) the reek of cheap rum. It were as if Daniel had been rolled in the soiled sheets of a brothel and dipped in the whores' latrine. It was the smell of immorality, decay, and death; Daniel carried it with him to bed every night. And despite the fact that I no longer kissed him (and we certainly never made love), his scent filled my days. I could taste it in food. My saliva seemed made of it. It somehow wafted from the television mid-movie, just as Clint Eastwood leaned in to kiss the female lead.

So let us suppose I discard blame, as Claudia recommends. The question remains: what made me do it?

Perhaps I thought things could be different for my daughter. Perhaps I thought she could avoid all the suffering I'd accepted as part and parcel of a young woman's life. Getting married to the first man who makes you feel beautiful. Carrying your firstborn into a world full of immorality and injustice. ~~But surely this does not justify murder, and that's the appropriate word for~~

Abilena was too headstrong to terminate the pregnancy on my orders alone. By the time I placed the box of pills on her nightstand, she'd already made her decision. I simply facilitated the inevitable, ensuring the act would be carried out with utmost safety. It was never my intention to spurn God's will. Was it not Him who made her the way she is? How much sorrow could have been avoided if some well-meaning hand had placed a similar box on my nightstand when the time came? If, as a result, William's wretched flesh had never seen the light of earthly existence?

The Kidney Bean (Age 17)

Nesto's paying me to cut the avocados lengthwise, but the knife's too fat and clumsy to avoid his yelling, and the flesh refuses to part when I slip my fingers beneath the skin. The avocado suffers but the strawberry at its core remains unblemished, as if it were razor-sliced by some unseen force. Miss Mendoza can see clearly. She can see the rabbit in the moon and the cunt in the strawberry. But ever since black friday we're the only ones still in business, and the old women line the road into the *barrio* to buy our miracle fruit. In exchange they bring valuables. Silver-framed pictures of their nephews and nieces. Flawless pearl necklaces hidden in soiled socks. Engagement rings. Wedding bands and their rough diamonds. Gold and silver watches engraved with initials in cursive. One *viejita* brings her dog, slits its neck, and presents us with its milky emerald eyes floating in a crystal chalice of velvety blood. Antique chairs. An oil painting of Simon Bolivar. One woman wears a copper necklace strung with the teeth of a yanomami indian. Another advances with the morion of a conquistador on her bald head. *Cáncer ovárico,* she whispers. I can barely hear her words above the commotion. Nesto's screaming to move faster, Abi! They keep coming! They just keep on coming! We're gonna be fucking rich! He places in their wrinkled hands a savaged avocado and it's spotless strawberry cunt. An army of *morochos* are working for us, carelessly walking in and out of our home with each item. They're clumsy as hell. The portrait's torn on a rusted nail. The chairs chip on the rough doorway. Pearls fall among the avocado skins and are lost in the pile. *Muévete,* Abi!

Let's keep it going! We're making a killing but it won't last forever! These old bitches'll starve penniless in the street before the sun goes down, and we'll still own the only tree in Caracas! I'm trying Nesto. I'm fucking trying. But I fumble with the dull knife and he keeps yelling. Abi! Abi! Abi, wake up.

You're sweating like a pig. Is everything ok?

I look at Bill. His pupils are enormous and he's smiling cause he knows the baby's gone.

You've been mumbling in your sleep for the last hour, *pequeña*.

I feel tired.

You slept pretty well. Most of the night.

You didnt' sleep?

Couldn't. Had to take care of you.

Bill's purple-rimmed eyes shining wet like a martyr's.

I'm so sorry about what happened yesterday, Abi.

Don't worry. I'll be fine, *flaco*.

I've made some eggs and bought bread. Want breakfast?

Sure. Just give me a second.

I stand up. My legs feel weak.

Can I take a shower?

Sure thing. Use any towel you want. The pink one's the least dirty.

Do you have soap?

Of course I have soap. Who do you think I am?

When I pull down my undies I notice the pad's barely stained. Bill must have changed it recently. I put my fingers inside and notice it among the pill fragments. A kidney bean. And so I watch it float in the toilet water. It'll be flushed into a field and some little girl will find it. She'll poke it with toothpicks and watch it grow. Then one day she'll wander to the bottom of the garden and push it into the soil. In a few years it'll become a man, a *morocho* with the soft brown skin of a kidney bean. And he'll have black bushy eyebrows and big brown eyes. So I flush the toilet and shower, making sure not to step on the *cucarachas* crawling the tile. Can't stand them usually, but right now the roaches just look like walking kidney beans. I take a fresh pair of underwear out of the bag and make sure the pad's in place. Then I get dressed and brush my teeth. The apartment looks even worse than I remember from last night. Bill's washed a couple plates and cleared the coffee table.

How do you feel?

Better. The eggs taste delicious.

Bill eats half of his and then sits back in his chair. He looks disgusted.

You gonna finish that?

Nope.

Can I have it?

Yeah, go ahead.

So I eat Bill's eggs too, mopping the yolk with pieces of bread.

Bill, when are you gonna come home?

Never.

You asshole.

Soon you'll leave for college, Abi. Maybe then you'll understand.

They can't afford to send me.

Well one day you'll have to grow up and find your own way, cause mom and dad sure as fuck won't do it for you.

What's your problem with the parents, Bill?

Nevermind that. Just try to stay realistic. You're gonna be an adult soon. Then nobody can tell you what to do.

You're one to talk, Bill. Is this what you wanna be doing? Living in this rathole in the *barrio* with *cucarachas* crawling in the mattress? Getting robbed by drug dealers in ski masks?

You came running pretty quickly when you wanted to get rid of your baby.

I never had a baby. It wasn't mine.

I'm just saying you're no saint.

I miss you Bill. I'm sorry. I just miss you lots.

I know, Abi. I miss you too.

Then why can't you stop doing this? Why can't you just find a way out?

I'm trying. It's not that simple.

It is simple. It's so goddamn simple. Come with me and we'll find a place near the beach. Let's get out of this city, Bill. I'm scared.

He laughs his sad laugh and grabs me by the scruff of the neck. Bill smells awful.

Abi, I'll be fine. Believe me.

I don't, Bill. I don't.

One day you'll see, Abi. We don't really have a choice. You go out there and be you. I'll be me. But stop worrying so fucking much. You keep worrying like this, you'll end up like mom.

So I can see Bill very far away, standing on the floating dock in the middle of the lake, and he's waving to the shore. But his eyes are little emeralds and he's covered in jewelry.

Please stop crying, Abi. Please.

I have to go to school, Bill.

Ok.

Here's the home number.

I already have it.

I just thought maybe you'd lost it or something.

No, I still have it, but I can't just

Put on a funny voice and ask for me. I won't tell them it's you. I'll tell them it's one of my dumb friends.

Ok.

I've tried to call, but your line never answers.

They took the phone, Abi.

Well then walk to a payphone, goddamnit. Walk to a fucking payphone, *rojo hijo de puta flaco de mierda.*

Sarah — April 21st, 1996

AFFIRMATIONS

I am one of the sisters.
It is not my venom I expel with these words.
I can rest safely in the compassionate arms of God.
My sisters are here to guide me.

Claudia is sitting next to me as I write these words. With her support I can become honest with myself about my past motives. In this way I will be forgiven and find compassion for myself.

THE TRUTH

- My facilitation of Abilena's abortion had nothing to do with increasing her freedom or autonomy. In my eyes she was a damaged woman, who at best might be afforded the same forgiveness God grants prostitutes.

- The real reason: I could not bear the thought of looking into the hateful eyes of a bastard grand-child, one I would never love. (Pale green irises just like William's, accusing me of unforgivable crimes, another miserable generation paying the price for the blood I carry, stained by history's darkest chapter, for which my family will suffer until our last descendant expires).

THE FRUIT OF MY PRACTICE

- Gratitude for my life as it exists today.

- An important role in this community. True sisterhood. A place for my dreadful thoughts to breathe and dissipate.

- The support of strong women who used to be everything from prostitutes to housewives. (Some were beaten severely by their husbands and, when they attempted to report these crimes, were accused by the police of lying or exaggerating. Others lost their minds and were forced into mental institutions by their "loved ones", where they were drugged, beaten and raped. Some were Child Prostitutes who's own fathers profited from their debasing. Many were assaulted in the street and then gang-raped by the police to whom they turned for protection. Thousands of these stories are being written each day. Mine pales in comparison. I have lived a privileged life.)

- These words could help another woman find hope if she reads them. Claudia says I write beautifully. Perhaps my education offers me a unique opportunity to be useful as an instrument of God.

Daniel — 22 of August of 1997

I remember the day Bill fell because I wasnt even that drunk. Sarah bought me a dozen polar the night before and told me to switch off the Rum. Kept telling me Abi was gonna wear a dress. DONT RUIN THIS ONE DANIEL. DONT RUIN THIS ONE. She kept screeching and nagging. So I stayed on the beer that night and the next day I only had a couple before the shindig. Took a couple sips of Rum in the kitchen when Sarah wasnt looking to fortefy myself. She wouldnt have understood. It was just to stop the shakes so I could tie my own bowtie. That day was a real scorcher too must have been 30 degrees out. My old suit was soked in sweat. It was the day we all got together to watch Nesto finally marry that quiet broad. The ceremony hapened at the same pavilion where me and Sarah tied the not and became husband and wife. It was a real beautiful place with a big balroom and a giant garden. It probably still is. That day almost felt like we were marying a child off. Always liked Nesto too. Thought he was good for Abi and her flites of fancy. Thought he helped her down to earth. A good boy. Sometimes even wondered. If Nesto were my son would I be proud of him and lay off the booze? HA HA HA. GIVE ME A BREAK OLD MAN. If Abilena didnt change me then nobody could. But it was a pretty ceremony. Exept when it went to shit on account of Billy being drunk as hell. I remember wondering if thats how I looked. Shameful really. Yes he was a good kid that Nesto and I bet hes got a good life now. Probably some kids with that girl. I wish Billy would have folowed the same road.

I wish he would have gotten on with his life after the usual partying and fucking around we all do when were young. But I guess Billy and me have that in common when it comes to partys. Always the first man falling and the last man standing.

Down from the Branch (Age 19)

A pattern of blood-red hibiscus on the day of Nesto's fucking wedding. An ugly dress covered in yellow-tipped stamen surging from red petals where insects crawl, and the dark aureoles where they fall to drown in sticky sweetness. It's not mine anyway. Mom said I looked beautiful, but I know she's lying cause it's too tight around the waist and I don't fill it well. I wore it as a young woman, she told me. Anyways you've ruined or lost all the dresses I've bought you. Beggars can't be choosers, Abilena. But I ignored her cause mom's always like that.

There's a crowd already, lounging in the wicker chairs with their moldy blue pillows. All it takes is a quick peek below and you'll see, the mold spreading into their freshly-pressed chinos to make their balls rotten, ageing men with their nasty cigars and crummy moustaches and pomade-slicked hair. The dregs of colonialism, hairlines receding into obscurity. And Bill can't sit still, so he's scuttling back and forth to the bathroom every few minutes.

Bill, just sit down, you're driving me nuts.

Abi, why're we here? Who gives a fuck about him anyway.

Bill taps his feet on the black and white checkered tile. I look around the ballroom. They must have paid plenty to string the garlands like that, all the way to the chandelier from every corner, its gleaming prisms drawing moths and mosquitoes into a desperate circle dance.

You look beautiful, *pequeña*.

Thanks Billy.

Let's go have a drink.

Bill.

What?

Let's just

C'mon Abi, loosen up. Who put a stick up your ass?

I've never had a drink in my life, Bill.

Jesus christ, Abi. That's insane.

Well dad

It'll help you get through the ceremony. Or we can leave.

No, I promised I'd be here.

Oh, who gives a shit what you promised.

I keep my promises.

Good for you. Now let's hit the wood bar.

That place depresses me.

Aren't you already depressed?

And with that he walks away, handsome in his all-white suit and skinny purple tie. Electric Bill you scrawny monster, shifting around like a pop star in your last days, dyeing everything black with those terrible green eyes and that cruel mouth. He spits in the grass and I navigate the concrete stairs in my awkward black pumps.

Wait for me, dickhead. I can't walk fast in these things.

Then take them off. You can clobber Nesto with them later.

You're awful.

Get real Abi. He's an asshole.

So I unstrap and walk the crabgrass, but Bill doesn't wait.

I need a fucking drink.

You always need a drink.

The bar's chipped malachite and varnished wood, reeking of old cigar stubs and pressed down by the low ceiling. Luxury pulverized and resculpted for the dead. The flimsy dartboards and moist felt, embalmed soccer jerseys behind yellow glass. Nothing's ever lived here.

I'll take a double whiskey on the rocks and she'll have a rum and pepsi.

Si, señor Bill. Bienvenido de vuelta.

I don't want rum.

But it's a good mix. *Cuba libre.*

I don't care. I don't want any rum.

She'll have a whiskey pepsi.

So one double whiskey on the rocks and a whiskey pepsi. *De acuerdo?*

Perfect. *Gracias, Gus.*

No problem, *señor Bill.* That'll be seventy *bolivares.*

Just put it on the account.

I can't, sir. I was instructed not to.

Are you fucking kidding me? I don't have any cash on me.

I'm sorry, sir, I just can't.

Bill reaches for his drink and puts most of it away in a couple of gulps. Gustavo doesn't try to stop him. The *morocho*'s expression is blank. When Bill puts the glass down, one of the cubes cracks in half.

How the fuck do two drinks cost fourty *bolos, Gus?*

Viernes negro, señor Bill. The whiskey's imported. *El mundo se fue al carajo.*

I've got money, Bill.

Abi, you don't need to

Just let me pay the man.

I can see the whiskey reach Bill cause he relaxes, fine with the dollars I pull out of my bra and hand to Gustavo.

Que mierda este pais, pequeña. The country's gone to shit.

Yes sir. Thank you, *señora.*

Señorita, por favor.

Of course, I'm sorry *señorita.*

I guess you're getting old, Abi.

Not as fast as you, *flaco.*

So I take a sip and it tastes of pepsi cola til it doesn't. Cause afterwards it goes down warm and cold at once.

Looks like you're enjoying it.

Tastes awful.

Bill puts his empty glass on the bar and starts tapping his knee with his fingers. He looks at my drink and looks at me.

It'll work though. Always does.

I close my eyes and feel the warmth, elbows propped on the bar, thinking of how cruel he is. This Bill. Remembering the day he shot the little bird right off the tree. When we were just kids. Look at that bird, *pequeña*, can you see it? I can see it, Bill, hopping up and down the branch, a small black shape against the bright blue. Don't Bill. Please don't. *Cálmate.* Relax. Bill shoulders the rifle and leans on the balcony with his bony elbows. Stop screaming, Abi. Shut up or I'll make you. Then he holds his breath and I hear the cracking snap of the bird disappearing from the tree. Why d'you do that, Bill? Why? The little bird. Shut up. Come with me! And he grabs my hand, sweating cold as he pulls me down the stairs and onto the patio. By the time we get to the bottom of the garden I can't see through my tears. Why, Bill? You. And Bill stops and looks. *La carpintera. La carpintera.* The woodpecker. With her red hat and yellow-black belly. She's breathing ragged through a bloody hole. Her heart's gonna die inside the feathers! Cause her heart's not working and the woodpecker looks wet and black with her shrimp eyes. And the bumping heart in the red bloody. Bump, bump, bump. Til it stops. But Bill don't move and his eyes don't move and he doesn't stop me when I pick up the dead birdy. Why did you. Oh Bill. But there's nothing nobody can do. Cause that bird died from Bill's goddamn rifle. Daddy never killed nobody, but Bill killed that bird, cause it can't lie when it dies in your hands. That's forever. Everyone knows it, you little twerp. He never killed those fucking chinks. He never even went to war. He was too young to be in Korea. Dad's a fucking liar. I kiss the bird softly and bury it in the grass. Sleep well, pretty lady. Keep your red hat on when you get to heaven. You'll be the best one. You'll show that slut she's playing second-fiddle. Cause Nesto's lost forever but only cause I didn't want him. So how could that be love? It wasn't. And there's no way to close a woodpecker's eyes like they do in the movies, so I bury it open-eyed in the soil. Won't be much to see down there anyway. And one day there'll be a tree of birds, each branch a wing, each fruit a moist black eyeball, each leaf a yellow feather. And a trunk of pure white bone to remember what Bill done.

I open my eyes again. The awful bar. Bill. He drinks all my dollars on the rocks and I knock back two more whiskey pepsis. Then he goes to the bathroom while Gus smiles like an idiot and I pull my dress up to stop the showing. Sweet Gus. I've got no tits to show you. Sweet little *morocho* like a caramel in the sun. I lean over the bar and kiss him on the mouth, but he stops smiling and the bottles jiggle behind him as he backs into the glass shelf.

Señorita. No puedo.

Then Bill comes out of the bathroom and grabs my

wrist and we walk up the steps as the ceremony begins in the grassy area next to the ballroom. Of course she's beautiful in white, cause she smiles at Nesto without pause, from behind the veil and after, and I can see she's truly filled with joy. He's handsome kissing her after the priest gives them his blessing. So today's right for everyone and his mother cries and mom and dad are smiling like I've never seen. Cause you can be happy when people are happy, and today we all have permission.

Bill pulls me onto the roof of the ballroom and I lose a shoe and don't go back for it. From up here we can see the people gathered on the grass in their black suits with bowties, short satin dresses and pretty hats. Bill has a little bottle of whiskey in his jacket so I have a sip from the warm moment on the roof. Nobody can see us up here, and Nesto's standing with his wife in front of the brick wall as the photographer directs them. We stand on the edge of the roof, directly above them and looking down on the happiness of others. Then Bill swivels

Fuck them anyway, Abi.

And he throws his head to drain the bottle and stumbles backwards, disappearing from the rooftop. Then the screaming of arms wrapped around women cause I know what happened. He broke his back on the brick wall, face upside down and blankly staring, draped unnaturally in frozen agony. Two men pull him to the grass and Nesto stands over Bill, who can't say nothing cause he's too white. Nothing's moving with Bill.

How could you not, you piece of shit! How could you not come ruin this day for me. Everything you do turns to shit, and here you are again, *hijo de puta*.

Nesto holds him by the blank drooling collar. Bill looks at him maliciously.

You fucking abandoned me, *amigo*. You left me out there alone. Too good for the fucking *barrio*, huh? I hope you're happy with your bride, you cocksucker.

I am, Bill. I don't give a shit what you think. You need to fucking grow up. There's more to life than drinking whiskey and sniffing coke, you fucking leper. Do yourself a favor and fucking die.

Bill's drooling blood on the white suit. Other men begin to intervene.

Let him go, Nesto. Can't you see he's hurt?

And two men carry Bill into the taxi. Nesto throws a few bills at the driver.

Lleva este hijo de puta al hospital. Get him out of my face.

From inside the cab, and I can't be sure, but I think I hear Bill's voice, caged and fading.

Did you enjoy my sister?

Then *merengue* plays over the crowd cause they stand

like fucking idiots, staring at the bride as Nesto walks past her to the bathroom. They'll be talking for months in the church parking lot, til I see mom and dad frozen pale against the palms. So I look at the broken flask on the green paint of the roof and lie down for a moment in the heat, the image of their horrified faces floating in and out of waves. Bill broke his back but they carried him into the taxi. Nobody went with him. And from our spines we stand against the waves, cause they'd shatter us into the sand if we let them. And some they do. But my dress is torn and they're shouting my name across the ballroom.

Abilena! Abilena!

Hello. I'm here.

Abi?

I'm right here.

Where?

On top. On the roof.

Oh thank god. What are you doing up there, Abi? We were worried sick! We found one of your shoes.

I told you she wasn't kidnapped.

Shut up, Danny.

Honey, please come down. It's late and it's time to

go home.

So I grab my pump and swing myself up and stand on my feet and step on the broken glass. It goes inside me, splitting my sole as I crumple in a heap.

Abi, are you alright? What happened?

I stepped on glass. Broken glass.

I'm coming up there.

The pain jabs into my foot and up my leg and I can barely breathe cause I'm clenching my teeth so hard.

Abi.

Daddy.

Look at you. You're drunk.

I know.

You look like something washed up on the beach.

I feel really bad. Where's Bill? What happened to

He's at the hospital.

Will he walk? Is he

Calm down, Bibi. We don't know yet. He's in good

hands. We can visit him tomorrow.

What's. And Billy. Oh Daddy. What's wrong with this family?

I have no idea.

Something's so, so wrong.

I don't know, Abi. I don't know.

Cause Dad's in a suit and not even sweet. Daniel was a quiet baby and a happy boy and an insolent young man.

I'm sorry, Abi.

It's ok, Dad. I'm just sweet. Can you carry me?

So Daniel leans down and grunts, pulling me close. When I was in the avocado tree he always knew where to find me. He would look up into the branches, one eye closed and squinting, but he never climbed up to get me, only smiled, cause Dad knew I was fine.

Daniel — 1 of September of 1997

Theres blood that bonds me and Abilena even though our lives are very diferent. Shes an artist and Im a fisherman. Fishing went to shit after black friday cause my money was worthless and the lake was getting blockaded by these gringos taking my business. They kept teling me to sell but I said no. Still had some contacts and was too proud to buckle. I mean they were in the bushes a lot outside the place. I can hear them sometimes even up here in the mountain with their silent riffles and their binoculars. If I go back to Caracas they would shoot me on site. The CIA cant read these words because I keep this book under my sleeping bag and always make sure theres no direct line of sight from the window. But the Americans have tecknology that can see through walls and read the heat in your body. They can stop your heart with electricity. But they cant read these words because their cold words written by a man whos already dead. Thats why they dont care about danny because danny doesnt even show up on the radars. Hes cold as a dead duck in a pond of ice. HA HA HA. If a man falls alone in a forest does he make a sound? If the CIA and the politicos inject you with truth drugs to make you talk but you have no mind and no heart then do they get anything from you? Do they torture you to death just for fun? Like the animals do to each other? YOUR GOING FUCKING CRAZY DANIEL. YOUR LOSING IT. FIND THE PLOT. FIND THE PLOT. Abilena. Think of Abilena. You were writing about Abilena and her ART. She made beautiful things. I didnt see it of course. I thought she was making a huge mistake. Money in ART? Not in South America. No way. What I didnt know is that making ART was like pick pocketing the aristocrats. Those cocksuckers bled the middle class and with the money they buyed paintings for insane amounts of money and hanging them on the walls of their third and fourth homes. Plus Bibi got paid in dollars so she was making a real killing because the bolivar was falling every day. Mamahuevos were standing outside the banks changing bolos cause they knew they could sell the dollars a week later and make money. I should have done that. If I wasnt so fucking proud. So it was a real busines this ART! But it wasnt just that. Abilena was really talented too. Her paintings were some of the most incredible things Ive ever seen. It wasnt that they looked real because she never drew the details like Da Vinci or those other Europeans did. She was more like PICASSO sort of in the way she made you feel. She painted with GUTS. Her portrates of people were REAL. I was proud of her and of the money she was making so I converted my office into an ART studio. I never used the room anyway exept for drinking alone. I payed for her paint and brushes and canvases and whatever she needed. She was sliping me money too. It helped us survive. I was so proud of her. Honest to god. But I was also diferent than her. Thats why. Because I was a fuckup then. AND NOW. One time Abi invited me to one of her ART shows. I promised her I wouldnt booze before. Just enough to be steady and good. Somehow I kept the promise to stay on the beers. But the show was hard. I was a guy strugling to make a buck and wearing his only suit and standing in the middle of a fancy ART show. They checked my identity card three times before letting me in because I was a FUCKING NIGGER to them. And inside it was just ladys with furs and jewels and high heels. Rich men colaborating with the CIA but never really working because they all had banana or sugar or rubber or aluminum or oil conections and they came to the ART show with their young whores. There was also queers and intelectual types. And me looking like a dumb fucking hick. I wanted to tell them that it was my daughter who made this ART. Your all here because my daughter made these and I was the one who made my daughter so FUCK YOU. What have you done with your lifes? Youv taken the money from the middle class and the pueblo and give nothing to nobody. YOU ARE SCUM. You work the pueblo into their grave. Your monsters. But I kept my mouth shut on account of Abi and her ART. Didn't want to embarras her. She didnt give 2 damns about them. She didnt dress up for them like a whore. She was beter than the rich. She wasnt a rich or a gringo or a queer or an intelectual or anything else. She was herself and only herself. She was wearing a simple cotton dress and sneekers. The ART show directer was this guy with 3 names. First he looked at me like I was dogshit he just steped in. Then he lernt out I was Abis father and his attitude changed. He wouldnt stop asking me if I had what I needed. DO YOU HAVE WHAT YOU NEED? DO YOU HAVE WHAT YOU NEED? He kept screeching over and over and over. He ment drinks of course but I still wanted to kill him. NO I DONT HAVE WHAT I NEED. I DONT KNOW WHAT I NEED. DO YOU? I know their watching me but thats because Im not fucking stupid neither. I know about how things hapen in the world. Everybody gets controled by something and if they cant control you they eat you insted. But I just shut up and drank the champane even though it tasted like shit. I fucking hate champane because it gives me a headache. It Doesnt get me drunk at all and its a useless fucking drink. The ceilings in the ART show were so high and the paint was so wite and it felt like we were in a dream. Maybe its stil a dream. It looked like heaven but the people belonged in hell. In the end it was a good thing if they paid Bibi and gave her money and told her nice things about her ART. Good because she deserved it. She wasnt ashamed of her father and were I came from. Im not rich. Then this fat guy with a moustache and cowboy boots walked his fucking whore up to the painting Bibi made of the indian kid. I remember he kept rubing his moustache like he was thinking about something real deep. The whore just looked bored. She must have been seventeen. But he asked her what does it make you feel? So she said I dont know. What do you mean you dont know? He asks her like shes not a whore. Its gotta make you feel something right? You do feel right? Sure I feel she said sounding a little mad too cause she was a whore but probably smarter than him. Well then what do you feel when your looking at the painting? He asked her again. I want to help him she said. He looks lonely she said. She was sounding sort of sad and pathetic when she said it to. NOT ABOUT THE FUCKING INDIAN ABOUT THE PAINTING he yelled at her. ABOUT THE PAINTING he said. I dont know she said and fiddled with her shoes. Its nice I guess. So then the rich guy just shakes his head as if to say these whores will never learn. Then finally he says really loud like everybody should be listening to him. WELL ITS DEFINITELY GOT SOMETHING. I CANT PERSONALY SEE IT AND I DONT LIKE IT BUT ITS GOT SOMETHING. Then he walked over to the next painting with the whore wobbling on her shoes as he held her up. After that I sort of felt better about the ART show. He was dumber than me that cocksucker. He was just like the gringos Id been ripping off for years. I was just passing on the family busines to Bibi. Somebody had to make money off these cocksuckers. The fishing was barely cutting it. In the low season I couldnt aford the monthly payments. We were surviving by the skin of my teeth. Maybe things for Bibi could be better. I wanted things to be good for her. Even though I was sinking I always was trying to push Bibi up up up to the surface.

Between Women and Ghosts (Age 22)

Abilena Heron is a brave young artist conjugating South American magic realism into the present tense. Her surreal and often jarring universe is built on the cultural tropes of the nuclear family in the neo-colonial era. As a humanist with genuine affection for all her subjects (whether real or imaginary), Abilena holds the promise of becoming a strong post-feminist voice in the contemporary South American art scene.

D o you like it, Abi?

I love it, Miss. It's a great introduction. Thanks so much for writing it. For everything really. This feels like a dream.

Abi, call me Carolina. Quit it with the Miss bullshit. You're not my student anymore.

And you don't think my fake name is stupid?

No, I don't. It's a great *nom de plume.* Now you gotta grow a fucking cunt and wear it with pride.

Ok. I'll put it on my list of things to do.

Abi, listen. This is your first solo expo. That means you're a real artist now. Not that you weren't one before. I've always known. But with these morons you gotta have a solo show before you become official. Now you have one.

But all these people

They're just people. Look around you. They all came to see your work.

They come to all the shows.

Not all the shows are as good as this one.

My eyes jump from one painting to the next. It's hard to focus. Miss Mendoza can tell I'm nervous, so she pushes me into a group of people and I spill someone's drink and they smile at me. I go to clean it up but there's already a waiter down there wiping the floor. There's a little gash of dried blood on the waiter's bald scalp. He keeps his eyes down.

That guy. The waiter. He's

Meet the artist!

They turn to me, all of them at once, especially a bearded man with salt and pepper hair smoking a cigarette through his yellow teeth.

Miss Heron, I presume.

Yes. You don't have to, um. You can just call me

Congratulations on your success. It's not every day such

a young artist gets backed by an adored member of our little family. *Nuestra pequeña familia.* And so charming too. So young. Such a fresh thing. Can we look at the paintings together? Come. I have a few questions.

And he touches my arm gently and I shudder til we stand in front of the old lady with the morion.

How do you explain your decision to paint her bald and naked? Is it a nod to the native resistance's scalping practices, or simply an unapologetic juxtaposition of the raw female form with a classic symbol of oppression?

And he smiles at me through his tortoise-shell rims. I don't say anything but in my head I can remember the dream so vividly, the old lady's eyes burning as she waited in line with her morion, to trade it for half an avocado from the only tree in town. I want to gut this man like a fish. I want to punch him in the eye for asking me questions. And what's the answer? She's there and now she's here, on the canvas? Who painted the painting I painted? But the man waits patiently cause I don't say anything. When I finally speak, my voice sounds alright after the first word.

I don't know.

And there's no pause cause he was just waiting for me to finish.

Interesting. You seem very fresh. That's good. So would you say it's part of the artist's role to smuggle subconscious thoughts past the left brain? Do you consider yourself a painter or a cook?

Well sometimes I like to cook, I guess.

Interesting, interesting. Yes.

But by the tone of his voice I know I've failed some kind of test. Miss Mendoza's standing beside me, holding my elbow too tightly. I don't even turn to her, cause I'm staring at the man, how his eyes keep darting back and forth between my mouth and neck. He licks his thin lips and Miss Mendoza starts whispering into my ear.

I bet you'd never met one in real life. He's a good introduction to their kind. Very polite for a mosquito. If he tries to fuck you he'll do it from behind so he can pretend you're a boy.

The man continues to smile at me, like a statue, but more grotesque and less beautiful. Miss Mendoza keeps whispering until I want her to shut up because her words are sharp and sweet. Instead of turning to her I find myself answering the man.

I don't really conceptualize the act of creation all that much. It's pretty simple. The images are there, in my mind, and the brush follows their shape as I look and feel. This happens until everything's right. Then it's time for the next painting.

Fascinating.

Miss Mendoza keeps whispering.

You're good. He doesn't know how to suck your blood. Watch what happens next.

The man doesn't move. Again he looks like some sort of statue or a mask in a horror film. His smile doesn't shift a bit.

Well, that's enough reductionism for a night. I must attend a summit in the little boys room. Excuse me, ladies.

He swivels around and places his empty glass onto a passing silver tray.

Who was that, Miss?

A critic.

Your friend?

Sure, why not. Come, let's move to the next painting. This is good for you. You're gonna have to learn to survive these things if you wanna get anywhere. Without sucking a prick of course. That's the goal.

Does it always feel like this?

Yes, but you'll get used to it.

I hope so.

You will, Abi. Just don't get married to any of them.

But even though my eyes are jumping around, I know the truth. Miss Mendoza's an ugly ghost. She learned joy from her own body, and happiness from a man, and when that man left her for another woman, Miss Mendoza found herself stranded outside of her own body. Cause joy exists naturally but happiness is the twin sister of suffering.

So Miss Mendoza carries her suffering from painting to painting, squeezing my fingers and smelling of champagne. The ceiling's a trellis of veins torn from an elephant's belly, bleeding into a chandelier made of pure ivory, its candles molded of white wax, but they don't melt cause their red flames cast a neutral light, and the champagne tastes of BB pellets.

I stop Miss Mendoza and hold her by the shoulders. She's magnificent with her tanned skin and shaved head, bright blue eyes with streaks of rust like bloody shoals pushing to the surface. Wrapped in a black judogi with a golden belt. And the surprise in her eyes. Cause I'm just a kid, but she knows that I know. And so I hold her in my arms, both of us very still, everything around us a chattering mess, her body loosening til I hold what she used to be. When it's over I can see her moist eyes thanking me and she drops her champagne into a garbage can and smiles.

I really like this one, Abi. It's so incredibly powerful.

I look up at the painting.

It reminds me so much of Frida Kahlo, but at the same time there's something in the girl's eyes that leaves no distance between her and the viewer. With Frida I always feel something holding me back. But not with this painting.

Thanks, Miss. It's hard for me to see anything when I look at it.

Miss Mendoza stands gazing at the painting before she turns to me and speaks.

Do you ever look at something you've created and wonder who made it?

All the time. That's why I didn't keep the baby, cause I'd probably make a shitty mother.

You were seventeen, Abi.

I know. I couldn't keep it anyway. Not with how I felt when I looked at Nesto. It really scared me. I could see he loved me, but there was just a wide, cold place where my feelings should have been. I didn't want my baby to wander that empty place with nothing to eat or drink.

Miss Mendoza squeezes my arm.

Abi, one day that place'll warm up. You won't even notice it. Then you'll know what it means be alive with another person. To share.

I look at Miss Mendoza and see a ghost. One day you'll wander the earth like me, the ghost says. Then Miss Mendoza speaks.

You think I don't know what you're thinking? You're a kid, Abi. You don't wanna end up like me. You look at me and you think something's broken. You'll never break. You'll be stronger. But just wait. Wait til you find someone that truly matters. It makes everything change. I'll be fine, Abi. I'll find my life again, or someone else to share with.

Miss Mendoza paces back and forth between two paintings and stops again to look at me, this time with wet eyes.

You probably think I'm a stupid old bitch.

No, I don't. I really don't. But I'm scared, Miss.

We all are. But the courage comes when it's needed. You'll be as stupid and brave as everyone else.

Her smile is broad and warm, cutting through my bullshit. Suddenly I'm aware that we're in an art gallery, surrounded by people.

You wanna know what my favorite painting is, Abi?

Yes, I do.

It's this one.

She points to Bill standing on the floating dock. His emerald eyes.

He's so far away, yet unbearably close. The way the jewelry hangs on his teenage body. I want to hold him, but he frightens me. I'm his mother and prey. That's what art should do, Abi. Allow impossible feelings to co-exist. Let me tell you something else, Abi. To be an artist is to watch things make themselves, just like the palm trees watch the waves hit the beach, or the sun watches the earth turn on its axis. So always remember to let things create themselves and enjoy them like you would a parrot or a skyscraper.

I'm trying to listen to Miss Mendoza, but I can barely breathe. The cigarette smoke hovers in fat coils above the liars, building steadily as they exhale. I push my way through the crowd, all of them turning to smile at me, to congratulate me, to ask me questions I'll never answer, to nod in agreement with Miss Mendoza and her ideas about art. Finally I step out of the gallery and find myself under the roiling sky, black and blue, disturbed only by a pale, clouded moon. Everything feels very far away. I'm alone. I stand for a long time waiting for nothing, looking mostly at the sky and seeing only a few stars. The night's humid when Connie finally arrives.

For a whole minute there's just a taxi with its door swung open, a cave entrance speckled with moth-shadows from the street lamp. Then the shifting light plays on her legs and face.

Keep the change.

Gracias, señorita.

And her eyes never leave mine as she lights a cigarette and pushes the pack into her blue jean cut-offs. Connie's black t-shirt look like it's been shredded by knives and her hair's in beautiful disorder. The smell of diesel exhaust as the moths beat themselves to the light. Her black leather heels.

Abi. La más linda.

So good to see you.

Y la más famosa.

She hugs me wide and warm like a sleeping bag on the football field. But Connie's drunker than I thought, kissing my neck and dragging her wet lips as she switches sides.

I can't believe you're exposing here. The most famous. My little Abi.

And before I can answer she slithers past me and into the building, her oily brown eyes slinking from shape to shape. Of course she knows some of them. Cause Connie's a dyke but she knows how to walk like an expensive prostitute. And after the day she kissed me, Connie got a boyfriend and went out dancing every night for a month. She moved in with him and didn't come to graduation. We never spoke about what she told me, and now she appears out of nowhere to smear my face with lipstick. I miss Connie cause she's a mess, always flooding the riverbanks with her black waters. But I also remember her simple face that day at school, and I miss my old friend Connie. So I follow her into the gallery but can't see her through the smoke, thicker than the paintings, rotting from the walls like teeth from a mouth. I wander the gallery for a bit, unable to find her again. Then Miss Mendoza tells me where Connie is. On her knees in a bathroom stall. She doesn't turn around when I speak to her.

You alright?

I'm fine. I'm fine.

You don't look fine.

Your paintings are really, really beautiful.

You'd seen them already.

Not all of them. I'd never seen that tree with the big. With those big black feathers. You know the one.

Yeah, that's the latest one I painted.

It's really fucking beautiful. That one.

And she vomits, the back of her knees contracting, gooseflesh on the back of her arms as she holds the toilet bowl, hair in a messy bun.

Connie.

I'll be fine. I'm fine.

Let me take you home.

Don't be mean to me. Princess Abi.

I'm never mean to you.

You know what I'm saying. You be a nice girl.

I'll call a cab.

I ruined your fucking expo.

No you didn't.

I fucking ruined it.

It's almost over.

Did you sell any paintings?

Two.

Amazing. So now you're rich and famous. A fucking artist. Everyone knows it. They're all talking about you.

I doubt it.

Oh come on. Enjoy yourself.

I talked to a guy from the MACC and he told me the museum might be interested in exposing them, so I might delay the sales.

Don't you need the money? What about the fucking money?

Maybe I can get a grant.

Fuck, Abi. You're so amazing. You're fucking great. I'm so impressed.

And Connie spits into the toilet bowl.

Ok, I'm ready to go. Let's go.

Can you walk?

Nope. You'll have to get one of your secretaries or agents or whatever. One of them to carry me.

I'll help you.

Mi hermana. We're like sisters. We can share anything.

We can tell it all to each other. You're so fucking cool. I ruined your expo. What're you gonna tell Miss Mendoza?

That you came to admit you're a lesbian and we're eloping to Rio to get married in the shadow of Christ the Redeemer.

What?

Nothing.

And so the smoke parts to let us pass, and we walk through the crowd, their heads turning to watch me carry Connie down the long corridor of paintings, faces contracting into questions and compliments and explanations, but I ignore them all. Miss Mendoza kisses Connie's forehead in benediction and the taxi's already out there when we clear the building, so we end up piling into the back seat, sticky where our bodies touch. The engine starts and the leather's humming and I feel warm and calm. Connie's asleep and snoring, shards of light snaking her body as we take sharp turns. Her breath smells like vinegar when I lean into it.

The driver is careless, jerking his old hands from left to right and chewing sunflower seeds. He flicks the spitty chunks into a popcan which he's shoved into a drink holder on the passenger side. He must've used a knife to slice the can open, cause I can see its edges gleaming intensely.

I look over at Connie. I know where we're heading

and I know it's gonna hurt . It's guaranteed with that mouth of hers, open like the bloody maw of a tigress gorged. But it doesn't matter cause I've already made my decision. There's something warm and hard behind my cunt where my gut tells me what to do. I'll carry it out cause Connie's beautiful and this *hijo de puta* is driving us in circles around *Prados Del Este* but I couldn't give a shit cause I know what's gonna happen next and it's not even a thought cause it's alive under my skin and it's part of my fucking body.

Sarah — June 22nd, 1996

Some decisions one makes without making. When I found the lump, I knew what it was. I knew the old family stories and I remembered, through the fuzzy lens of childhood, the sinister pallor of *Oma*'s face in those last months before she passed away. And when the second one appeared in my other breast, no space remained for doubt. But I was secretly grateful. Without knowing it, I had convened with my inner-most self and decided to die. If one is Catholic, one does not consider suicide. One simply allows God's will to take its course. It would not be a graceful exit, but by then I had given up on such notions of propriety. There would be no audience anyway. Daniel was roaring drunk (as usual) and rarely home to boot. When my husband did design to show his face he invariably reeked of spirits and other women. William was at the beach recovering from his injury, having denied his father and I visitation rights during his stint at the hospital. (This enraged Daniel, who barely agreed to foot the bill for William's operation. It was a miracle, the doctor informed us, that my son was not paralyzed after having been driven to the hospital in the back of a car.) Abilena made it abundantly clear that her mother was not high on her list of priorities (Oh how I wanted to tell her about the Cancer, just to see the look on her face, but I was scared she might alert the others and force me to seek treatment).

Left alone in the house with my burgeoning lumps, I even ceased playing bridge. All I did was eat and watch movies. It barely bothered me when I found spots of dried blood on the betamax labels. My few friends grew increasingly worried and sent the local pastor on a mission to shake me from my torpor. It was upon seeing the concern and compassion on that man's face that I became conscious of my death-wish. The next day I made an appointment with a specialist and began attending Pastor Jimenez's services.

Coño (Age 22)

I lay Connie on her bed and drink from a bottle in the cupboard. Brave now, I strip you of your clothing and sit on the bed, gazing at what makes them all crazy. I touch your stomach and your breasts, rising and falling heavy and brown. And there's that smell again, the way the underwear's yours, and the apartment too, and everything else for a mile in all directions.

Growing up, your mom didn't give a shit and nobody really knew where your dad was until he appeared on a deck chair by the pool, but neither of those fuckers could sully you. And when you let the boys touch you in the bathroom they all burned their fingertips on the white heat of your cunt. I watched you drive many teachers to tears by smiling when they slapped you and smiling when they slapped you again. You had a way of making them all fascists, cause you're living proof that nothing can change a person except a knife or a gun.

So I watch you naked and sleeping on the bed, not speaking nor moving, and I can feel the warm liquor making its choices. You're just a simple magic trick, Connie. Animated flesh. Brown and smooth with your perfect skin and vulgar little belly. So I walk you into the shower and run water down your breasts and into the crook of your pubis, trickling from the black bush, trickling from your chin, trickling from the tips of your fingers. I wonder how you taste Connie. When you're not here and your body's an empty home that I can wander from room to room. So after toweling your knees.

They're darker than the rest. Some parts are darker. So after toweling your feet, I lay your hair on the pillow, wet and winding black, and run my fingers along the proud black hair of your pits. Then I push one knee to the side, unraveling your flesh. First my fingers, then my lips. And your taste like gutter rain. And your smell like burnt pinewood.

My face is close to yours when your hands grip fiercely, pulling the back of my neck down into a sudden kiss. And your eyes never open. But torn from me the dress by those strong fingers. Black lava, black powder, black lining every edge. Black chalk in the brown mud. Hands everyplace. Torn open like a market to the sky. Fat black rain down the brown mud tunnels.

You come in growls, loud enough for the neighbors to hear, and laugh til I'm scared of how dark it's become. Then you rise suddenly and slam the door to the bathroom, pissing louder than a passing truck. I hear you spit in the toilet bowl and flush. A long silence follows, during which I slowly doze off. In my dream I'm small again, pretending to sleep as Dad sings to me from the doorway. Can see his black silhouette inside the golden rectangle, sweet and swaying. *Yo no soy marinero, soy capitán, soy capitán. Ah, la bamba. Ah, la bamba.*

By the time Connie comes back to bed, I know I've made a mistake, but it's too late now. You're awake and nothing can stop you. As if the jungle lifted me whole, the way your branches brace me up and bind my arms. The way you wrap around my belly like a snake. Cause the jungle floor's crawling with life and never goes dry, it'll swallow me whole if I let it. And when the storm finally whips the canopy wide, nobody mourns the split branches and torn trunks, the singed leaves and charred bark. My spine's turned to hot oil and my limbs convulse furiously as I come. Then we both lie in bed silently, and I can hear Connie's breathing. We'll bleed tomorrow, *hermana*.

Once the moon rises over the black beach, the silver tide recedes to reveal a dreamless sleep.

Mañana (Age 22)

In the morning she's a rat beneath the talon, her eyes wide and helpless. Connie wears cotton underwear and a checkered shirt, smiling flimsily as she fries eggs in the kitchen. I find the tampon at the bottom of my purse and push it in. No blood yet, but I know it's coming. And the sun's so bright it casts golden through the gloom of crumpled clothes and dirty dishes. But still the knot in my stomach won't go away, cause I've gotta talk to her now or never. It'll be worse tomorrow and bad the next day.

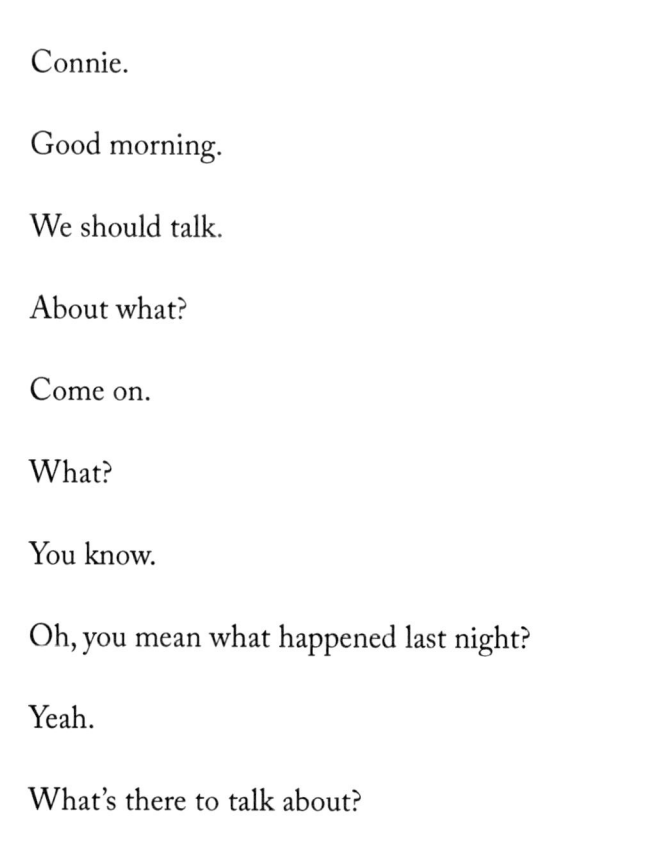

Connie.

Good morning.

We should talk.

About what?

Come on.

What?

You know.

Oh, you mean what happened last night?

Yeah.

What's there to talk about?

I don't wanna give you the wrong idea.

I'm not sure what you're talking about, Abi. I have a fucking boyfriend.

Right.

And the sound of plastic scraping the pan. Connie looks at the eggs.

So don't worry about it.

Connie, come on, you don't need to fool me.

Fuck you, Abi. Any moron can tell what I want. But you and me, we know it's never gonna happen. So why the fuck would I talk to you about it? Or do you just want me to be the one who cries for once?

I'm sorry. I just thought maybe. If you. Cause there's plenty of wonderful people out there.

Well that'll have to wait, Abi. Cause I'm a fucking coward. And you know it. But nobody else does. So just let me be. Let me keep the life I have.

Ok.

And so we sit down to eat the eggs. They're warm as the sun goes from yellow to white. A single fly cruises the dirty dishes. And Connie looks up with a crooked smile.

But maybe you could let me finger you on the weekends, *puta sucia*.

DANIEL — 83 of SEPTEMBER of 199

DOG IS TALKING TO ME. HE TELLING ME THAT CENTRAL BANK IS ALSO CENTRAL INTELIGENCE AGENCY. CB = CIA = BL = IMF = USA = $. THE BUFFALO COLABORATED WITH THE GRINGOS FROM THE START. HERRERA AND THE BUFFALO LEOPOLDO DIAZ BRUZUAL HIS WHITE BEARD AND BLACK EYES PRESSING ME DOWN FOR DAYS. WHEN I SIT AGAINST THE WALL SO THE RADIATION DOESNT REACH ME THEY MAKE IT TO THE VEGETABLES SO THE VEGETABLES ARE THINER AND POISON FOR ME. I AM THINER AND OLDER BECAUSE THE SKIN GOES FIRST. THE BUFFALO WAS ONE OF THEM AND KNEW ABOUT IT ALL. THEN CALDERA SAID YES TO THE IMF? THEY ALWAYS END UP GETING TO YOU. CALDERA WAS POISONED TO. JUST LIKE ME. THEY GRANTED AMESTY TO CHAVEZ CAUSE THEY PROBALY RADIATED HIS JAIL AND MADE HIM ALSO POISONED. $$$ POISONS EVERYTHING. $$$ POISONS THE WATER. DOG KNOWS IT. DOG KNOWS

Drifting (Age 23)

They found you in the crib, surrounded by toys and smiling. So they asked me, William, why are your toys in Abilena's crib? And I told them I didn't know. But a few days later it happened again. And still I wouldn't admit it. After about a month of this, mom walked in and caught me red-handed. I was standing over the crib, holding a plastic truck and aiming for your head. So she took me aside and had a talk with me. I know you're just playing William, but you could bruise Abilena with those toys. They're hard and sharp. And I just looked at her stupid face. She must've known. That's why she never told dad. Cause he would've let me have it. But she started keeping an eye on me. She thought I didn't understand what I was doing. But I understood, Abi. That's the awful part. I wanted to get rid of you. I wanted you gone.

So what, Bill? You were jealous of your younger sibling. That's really common for kids.

Bill's skin gets paler and his green eyes flare.

I just think there's something wrong with me.

Nothing's wrong, Bill. We're at the beach house, just the two of us. Can't you just enjoy it? Is it cause of the crutches?

Abi, let me tell you something about the crutches.

He leans in to whisper.

I don't need them.

Then why are you using them?

Cause I can't go back to the *barrio*, *pequeña*. There's some things happening there.

You owe people money.

Some things.

So you're just gonna stay on those crutches til you get old and the drug dealers kill each other?

I don't know, *pequeña*. I don't wanna go back to living with mom and dad in *El Peñon* either.

Why not?

Bill sighs.

Sometimes I wonder if we were born in the same family. Don't you think it's weird you still live with them?

They give me privacy.

Do they? Is that what you call it when mom sits with her videos and dad passes out drunk? Why do you think I drink all the time, Abi? Do you think all men just drink themselves to death? As much as I fucking hate Nesto, the only reason you left him is cause he's a decent guy. It must've been confusing for you.

You're such a fucking asshole, Bill.

I'm sorry *pequeña*, but it's true.

Go fuck yourself, Bill.

We sit in silence until I speak.

Are we gonna go to the beach or not?

Do you know if Modesto's around?

I saw him earlier this morning, watering the plants.

I think dad asked him to keep an eye on me.

Bill. You're crazy. Nobody's spying on you.

I wish it were that simple, Abi. But the world's pretty fucked up.

I don't want to live in your world, Bill. Maybe I'm delusional, but I'd rather stay this way than be suspicious all the time.

Suit yourself.

Can we go swimming now?

I don't know. If they see me swimming I'm in deep shit.

Billy, his car's gone. Nobody's around. We're the only ones here.

Fine. I'll bring the crutches with me just in case.

So we walk on the hot sand and leave Bill's crutches in the shade of a palm tree. Then we swim in silence to the first sandbar.

You're almost as tall as me. I can't believe it. I shouldn't call you *pequeña* anymore.

But I like it when you do.

Then I'll keep doing it.

You look a lot better, Bill.

Than when?

Than when I came to visit you in the *barrio*. Than the day of the wedding. Than the hospital.

I've never been out here without the parents. Haven't been drinking much. Just a little in the evening to relax. And they don't have all the awful stuff here.

The water breaks just inland of us, long and flat and rippling to the beach. Sun smoldering in the unbroken blue. Bodies slack above the sandbar, jumping again and again, buoyed effortlessly in the swell. Palm trees lining the distance, immobile as we drift the coast til we can't see the compound anymore.

Should we swim back?

Sure.

You look a little red.

I forgot to put sunscreen on.

Aren't you gonna die?

Probably.

And we walk the shoreline side by side, legs in rhythm as best I can. Bill's very long.

I'm hungry.

Me too.

What for?

Anything but shrimp.

Chipi-chipis?

No. Let's go get *arepas con jamón y queso*.

Ok.

Eggs (Age 23)

I make sure there's no sand in my toes by rubbing them together, then lie on the flimsy mattress and stare at the saltcrust ceiling and the wooden fan with its patches of mold spinning in blue orbits. It's worth letting it creak cause the noise is bad but the heat's worse. Nothing's worse than sweat in the sheets. So I leave one leg out and keep one leg in. Then I leave both legs out. Finally I push the sheet aside and lie flat on my back. With both eyes closed I hear the conversation between the artists again. Her paintings are very embryonic. What does that mean? They're undeveloped. Inchoate. Childish. You're right. Oh, hey Abilena. We were just talking about you. Inchoate. Oh hey. Very embryonic. You're right about that. Oh hey Abilena. Her paintings. Oh. Abilena. We were just.

In my dream Bill's face rises from the laguna. His sockets are muddy pools filled with shrimp. Then I see his wrists like red troughs filled with the yellow brown eggs of the red heron and the green eggs of the heron and the chalk-white eggs of the flamingo. Eggs bobbing in the warm blood. And his mouth spits up a geyser of rotten shrimp that disappears into the clouds, making them heavy and brown and ominous. And that's when he speaks. But not really words. More like a thick chanting. But I understand him. Cause life's not easy when you're William. And Janis did it. Not on purpose, but she did it. But Bill didn't do it. No he didn't. No you didn't. Promise me you won't. You gotta stay alive despite. You gotta. Promise me. But the crabs have gathered shoddy on the rim of the lagoon, clicking their awful claws to mourn the death of their king.

Sarah — June 25th 1996

Was it God or Satan who spoke through my child?

AFFIRMATIONS
Everything happens for a reason.
Sometimes it is not immediately apparent.
~~My son~~

Family Vacation (Age 23)

There's no music on the way to *Boca de Uchire* and nobody says anything. I stare out of the car window at the *ávila*, it's leathery talons of brown vegetation winding straight into the earth as we drive til night falls and then more The wind's really whipping dad's cigarette smoke in circles around the back seat, and I can't tell if mom's asleep or awake. I'm in the back seat thinking bout how she hid it so well. I never had any suspicions. No dreams either. One day she just came home with a flat chest made of hard bone and went about cooking dinner like nothing had changed.

Mom.

Yes, Abi?

What did you do?

Oh this? It's just temporary. I'll get a prosthesis soon enough.

Are you fucking crazy?

Please don't swear in front of your mother. Must I remind you that I'm not just one of your friends, Abi?

You have no breasts, mom. Don't you think you could stop what you're doing for a second and explain this to me?

She smiled and stared at me for a long time before she sat down at the dinner table. Dad wasn't home yet and I felt like I was in a bad school play.

I had a double mastectomy.

That's what they call it?

Yes.

I had a tumor in both of my breasts. But I knew what I had to do. This family needs me. So I eliminated the risk. But I'm aware it can look strange, so I'm going to get a prosthesis tomorrow.

Are you gonna tell dad?

I spoke to him on the phone today.

What did he say?

When you're in a marriage for a long time, things are a bit different. We're not young anymore, Abi. Some things have stopped mattering.

Did he know you had cancer?

More or less. But it's gone now. So it's good news, really. We can move on to more interesting things.

I wish you would've told me earlier.

I didn't want to worry you.

Still. I don't think it's right. You shouldn't have to go through this alone. I would've come with you to the hospital.

Some things we have to face alone. Life isn't always fun, Abi.

And so a few days later we're driving to the beach to visit Bill and she's sleeping in the front seat and dad's behind the wheel. The rain is falling hard, whipped skyward by the tires, glowing in the endless row of red taillights skirting the winding foothills in the warm wet dusk. And the plantain salesmen. And the peanut salesmen. Huddled together under plastic tarps on the roadside. And the wet green mangle of trees and vines. And the dead water rat with its guts burst open and beaten grey by the rain. And the torn metal wreckage of some deadly collision. Cause we're heading there, no choice, drawn together like a pile of marbles on a blanket. Into Bill's terrible trap.

Breaking Strength (Age 23)

It sure looks solid to me. Cause it's brown, not red, like mud softened by the rain and baked stiff by the sun. That's why I'm surprised when my fingers push right through. Cause it's still warm. I take my fingers out of the bathwater and wipe them on my jeans. When the flecks are in the water and the water dries, then the flecks are still there. That's how paint works. That's how you can take something and paint from it. Cause the real world hides inside the liquid. And the truth's absolutely pale. Dreams are lies. And the meat makes up the blood. He must've eaten plenty meat when I entered the beach house.

I was dripping wet after the short walk from the car. The storm had kicked over the little huts and torn the palms up.

I saw dad's fingers fumbling with the keys. And the kitchen with no change whatsoever. Cleaner mostly, with the plastic box and its dangling rows of knives and spoons and forks. And the wooden slats of the cabinets, one of them missing. The floor was white tile. Three of the tiles were cracked. I didn't step on any of them. But I could see the thin yellow sliver of light cast below the bathroom door. That's why I turned the knob slowly. And there were several things in the bathroom too. I was there. And the grimy old sponge was there beside the pale green soapbar. And the mirror above the sink, half-open cause I gotta close it and gather the hair in the sink too cause he shaved but didn't clean up after himself. And the crumpled yellow towel on the bathroom floor. And the tub with its orange soapstains like rectangles on rectangles. And Bill's hair, wet and pointing down over his closed eyes. He's actually tilted slightly out of the water, the back of his head pressed to the tile. Knees like springs, making sure he doesn't dip entirely, and wrists below the surface, dyeing the waters with their steady work. And so's the knife. And so's everything below the clavicle. And so's the red hair above his penis. I dip my fingers in the water. Can't even wander to his wrists. Nothing wrong with his

And Bill's in the bathroom. And I'm in the bathroom. There are several things in the bathroom. Before everything falls. And when it does I can tell my heart was there the entire time, drumming in the distance.

Bill. Bill.

Is he breathing to the drum of his breathing? I smear his nostrils with the blood of my fingers trying to see if he's breathing. I can hear loud breathing. Then I touch his face and touch his face and slap his face and it's my breathing. I slip on the edge of the tub when dad reaches through the impossible blood, stained past the elbow, to push his fingers under Bill's armpits and pull him out, like a puppet or a doll. Just straight down with no effort.

Do you got him, daddy. Do you

I got him.

What's that alarm, somebody should turn that alarm off. It's bursting my fucking ears that. He's naked streaming blood in cakes, dark where it used to be, red where it is.

For god's sake will you stop yelling, Bibi. Stop yelling and get me a couple of t-shirts.

So I'm in the bedroom looking. There's no t-shirts in the closet. There's a pair of pants but they're suit pants. There's no t-shirts in the closet. There's nothing but piles of dirty clothes on the floor.

Bibi. Anything. Move it.

Dad rips it into strips and ties the strips just past Billy's elbows, hard as possible. Now there's a white arm with a pink rim and the palest forearm with perfect gashes, over and over in a long set of crimson purposes.

Bibi. Bibi. Put the phone down. Fuck the ambulance. Let's take him in the car. Open the door, Abilena. Open the goddamn door. Don't just stand there.

So I sit in the back with Bill and we drive to the hospital without headlights or words or thoughts. Just Bill in the back, naked except for his strips. And he doesn't say nothing either. His mouth slightly open. If he drools it would pool in his clavicles. Then it would mix with the new blood.

Why'd they paint him so? Why'd his penis? Why'd the spots? How'd his hair get wet? Must've been the sink. But the road's humming into the wheels and the wheels're humming into the spokes and the spokes're humming into the frame and the frame's humming into the seat and the seat's humming into the strips. But they're fine. Tight as ever. We'll just tie him back to life.

As we drive to the hospital I go black and see Bill on his floating dock. The lake's a river and the dock's floating along in the rushing water. I run along the bank trying to get his attention.

Bill Bill Bill Bill Bill Bill Bill

but this time he don't answer

Bill Bill Bill Bill Bill Bill

but no answer. Then I gotta watch out cause the river's splitting wide and the grass gets torn from the banks. And soon I can see the curve ahead and realize immediately. It's a delta. It's a delta where the fresh and salt water mix. Where the river gets bigger til it spits out into the ocean and gets lost forever. To the thrashing

Bill Bill Bill Bill. Not out there. Don't you let it. Don't you let it take you. Don't you wanna stay with me and we'll move. Bill, we'll move to another country, far from the *barrio* and the parents and everything that makes you sick. You were born pure and they made you sick with their selves. You were born to exist somewhere with me.

Oh Bill.

Stop hitting him Abi. Stop it. You're not helping. Look at me.

Daddy daddy daddy

You've gotta be brave. You've gotta shut up now. We're almost there. *Pendejo*! Drive motherfucker! Get the fuck out of the way!

Turn there!

It's here.

Cause the motor chokes and the car door swings open. Soon the air sucks Bill into daddy's arms and he gets carried into the hospital, a beach hospital. Lots gone from Bill. I can tell cause he looks extra white. It always runs til its done, that's what water does. That's what blood does. So I'm standing on the shore and yelling out into the ocean.

Bill Bill Bill

Come on Abi. They've got him. They're gonna take care of him. He's in good hands. I know these guys. He'll be fine.

But the water foams in layers and the wind shifts across the salt-grey sky. The clouds are white and grey and darkening by the second. Can't tell the sea from the sky. Can't tell the waves from the clouds. Just a thick turbulence, a thick grey mire with William's floating dock at the center, receding into the distance. We're in the hospital and they've got Bill in the emergency room and I can hear em yelling. Nurses and doctors them. Mom's crying. She's sitting far away, face mashed with grief. I put my hand on her knee.

Mom, you're squeezing too hard.

But she can't hear me. And I didn't say it. Squeezing to the bone. If he cut himself lengthwise with the knife. Bill used the knife on his wrists. He must've made a mistake though. Cause Bill still wants to live. So he took the bath. But before the bath he wet his hair. Or he wet his hair in the bath and then sat up, locked his legs, and slit his wrists with the knife. That way the hair doesn't get bloody. And the face doesn't get bloody. But he still ends up in a bathtub full of blood like I found him. He was waiting for me to show up. Just dreamy and whispering my name. But I was looking at the dreams. So I'm the one with mud-filled eyes. I'm the blind one. It's my fault I couldn't save Bill.

Don't you start talking like that. Don't you start saying those things. You can't do nothing now. You can't do a goddamn thing for Bill. You start talking like that and there's no telling. So stop now and stop clean. Cause Abilena's a woman. She's a woman sitting in the hallway. And she's holding her mother's hand. Cause daddy's smoking outside. They told him, *señor, no se puede fumar aqui.* This is a hospital. So it's a promise. No matter what happens. We'll move far away from all this. We'll run from this rotten city and never look back. And we'll bring Connie too. And dad. And mom.

Bill you'd like Connie. Cept for what she did at the party. Cept for that. Cause it was her birthday. It was Connie's birthday. Right after the morning we fucked. There were plenty of drinks that night. Rodrigo had taken acid and cracked a glowstick into his hair. It dribbled into his eyes and made them red and blind and he wandered round screaming and laughing. Kept saying

Sparkle! Sparkle!

Fucking Rodrigo. Somebody take care of this moron. But there were too many people on acid and others were stoned. I was fine. Just had a couple drinks. So Connie wasn't looking at my eyes, just kept shifting from room to room, drinking too fast and smoking joints. Til she didn't look too happy, just sorta tired and mean. But in that way where I knew something bad was gonna happen. I was bracing for it, my ribs hard and aching. Cause she didn't care if she cared. Could see it in her red eyes. And she was sweet as hell.

So she grabbed Titi by the waist, and Titi loved it of course, cause Connie's so goddamn beautiful, and Titi's always sweet as hell with her dumb cunt slipping everywhere. Some people are always wet and they're just holes waiting to be filled. Their eyes scream out for Connie, cause she's trying to hurt me. How did I know, Bill? How did I know she was trying to hurt me. It was her eyes, Bill. Her goddamn eyes told me so. They looked over Titi's shoulder as she pushed down Titi's panties and Titi started shivering dumb with her little face buried in Connie's neck. She got caught on the hook. Like a wet fish squealing for life.

Sometimes when you touch them, some of them, they're just shaking and shaking. Like their parts aren't built very close together. Like there's so much loose space inside them, waiting to be filled. And their life's in your hands. Cause once you hook them they'll wriggle til the hook goes deeper and deeper as they struggle. Til finally their heart stops for a single moment. For some it's the only real thing they'll ever experience in their worthless lives, and they're silent even, reverent suddenly, like they realize all the talking was for nothing, cept moments later they're blabbing again like it never happened. But I know. And they know. Somewhere under all that noise, their body knows. Then you just wanna get rid of em.

Poor dumb Titi gets dragged right into the bedroom, heels tilted above the carpet. And Connie closes the door. But there's a little wet fire in the wood, making me dry on the inside. And my heart's broken. Not cause I love you, Connie, but I sure do love you, Connie. And you hurt me like this. Nothing like those eyes. Cause they say. I'm doing this to hurt you. Fuck you, Abilena. So I knew what it meant. And I sat with my empty glass on the stool near the door. Just waiting. Not waiting. Just sitting. Not sitting, just stunned. Not stunned, just absent. Just drying up. Til you opened that door and I could see Titi's naked body on the bed, sleeping in a clumsy heap.

And you were naked and crying, so beautiful in black and brown, so fertile and open. Like a pregnant child. Carrying the burden of your life one last stretch before you laid it down at my feet, sobbing and explaining it all.

I couldn't, Abi. But I did. I thought of you. Closed my eyes and thought of you. It was terrible. And I don't know what to do. I love you so much. I don't wanna lose what we have. But I don't know what I'm doing. I feel like a fucking whore. Cause her body's not your body, Abi. Her body's just a strange place I don't wanna explore.

I held Connie's head against my chest as she sat on my lap.

It's ok. Titi's fine. You're just all messed up. But nothing's broken. I'm right here.

Thank god for you, Abi. Thank god. You're just the loveliest, and I'm a fucking idiot.

No you're not. You're just learning about all this, like everybody else. If anyone's an idiot here, it's Rodrigo. He's literally screaming and stumbling over furniture.

And through her tears Connie laughed, and I knew it would be fine.

But I like girls.

I know.

A lot.

I know.

And I fell in love with my best friend.

I know.

And she doesn't love me.

I do.

But not like that.

No, not like that.

So I should just kill myself.

I'd rather you not.

But it hurts and I'm scared.

You'll be fine. You're just drunk.

And she sniffed and shook a little in my arms til she was asleep and I put her to bed and called a cab for Titi and told everyone to get the fuck out and take that asshole Rodrigo with you. So they did. And I held Connie. Cause she slept fine.

Cept Bill really did kill himself, right? Cause you can't just

And dad's back from his cigarette, leaning against the hospital wall. And mom stops crying. And we listen carefully to what the doctor says.

Sarah — July 3rd, 1996

When William was about three years old, Daniel and I brought him to a fancy theatre in downtown Caracas to watch The Sword and the Stone, his first movie. He screamed with joy at every scene and we were almost asked to leave several times. The usher eventually left us alone after Daniel threatened him physically. Once the film ended, we made our way towards the exit, and that's when William suddenly vanished into the crowd. We frantically asked the indifferent throng if they had spotted a small boy with red hair and green eyes, but nobody had seen him. He was gone. Daniel was so upset he could barely light a cigarette. After quite a bit of searching, we finally found William at a local *arepera*. He was chatting happily with a middle-aged British couple on vacation. They had bought him *churros*. Daniel wept with joy, holding William's face and kissing his forehead in rapture. I still remember the moment as if it were yesterday.

Daniel — 26 of October of 1997

I lost Billy. Sarah and I were leaving a shoping mall in the city. He was 3 years old. I let go of his hand for a second to lite a cigarette. He was gone when I reached back down for him. Sarah was crying and going on. I kept telling her to stop it with her screeching and nagging because I know my boy and he didnt go far so dont fucking worry woman. After about 5 minutes of looking we came across the kid. Hed found himself a couple of peruvianos who were having a beer after a long days work and they gave him some churros. Billy was happy as a fool sitting next to them. HA HA HA. Having caused his mother a fucking haert attack. I gave him something to think about. He spiled his churro and the boy was crying but sometimes a boy needs to learn a lesson to become a man and face the world because its a motherfucker of a place. I dont care what their teaching in sckools these days. You gotta be tougher than nails. Anyways there wasnt none of the fucking churro left because he had already stufed his little face. No harm no foul. My dad did much worse to me. Every genaration gets softer and the wolfs are waiting to eat them up. The dog died today. He shat all over the floor of the shack and I cleaned it up and the dog too. The surveilants went back to hiding themselfs because they think Im dead. No radiation since the dog died. Vegetables are still tasting strange so I puled them out and buried them far from the shack. Thats ok I have energy from the minerals in the rainwater. A new genaration is being born and Im gona be the guinee pig as usual so Ive acepted this. When I die theyl put my brain in a bomb to kil chavez who will be the first real president who doesnt lick the gringo boots. Ill try to turn it around and aim it at the white house. Nobody dies clean. I saw the dog and I know Ill be a tool for the gringos too. Is it a coincidens that dogs snif bombs? No. The animals know. It was a coup detat and it wont be the last. Thats why we put puppys in bags and drown them in the river or freez them in freezers. Cause they know whats good for them and they snif around too much and cause trouble.

Pancakes (Age 24)

Dad's lying face-down on the kitchen floor. He's wearing a pale blue shirt and khaki pants with no socks or belt.

Better not wake him, so I step around his body to open the wooden cabinet and reach for the frying pan. A glass of rum sits on the counter, capped by a thin film of thawed ice. I place the frying pan on the bottom right burner, the reliable one. There's seven matches left and the first two don't catch so I hold the third to the burner and twist the gas slowly, careful to keep my hair tucked behind my ears. Then I tiptoe around him again and reach into the yellow fridge for milk. Equal parts milk and water from the tap. Rinse the whisk til the grime's gone and beat the hell out of Aunt Jemima with equal parts milk and water. Cause I forgot the butter. So he moves a little, groaning as I reach into the fridge. I'd leave it out, but dad doesn't like the look of melting butter under glass, so we keep it in the fridge.

By the time the third pancake's stacked in the oven, I can hear mom's feet slapping up the stairs. Caught in the morning draught, her billowing white gown changes shapes like a jellyfish until she reaches the kitchen door and it settles to reveal her stubborn flat chest. She wears her sternum like a hard-earned medal.

Good morning gorgeous.

Morning, mom.

What a beautiful day.

She steps around dad and heads into the dining room.

I'm making pancakes.

I saw.

Have a seat. I set the table.

How wonderful.

Two or three?

Two's fine. Why don't you join me and eat while they're still warm?

What about him?

Who knows. I've rarely seen him rise in an eating mood.

How late did he stay up?

No idea.

They're good.

It's the syrup. Real maple syrup.

I don't know how we can afford that.

I pitch in. You know things are going well with the galleries.

I don't know how we can afford that, Abilena.

Did you sleep well?

I think so. Where's that breeze coming from? It's bloody freezing.

I walk over to the sliding doors and roll them shut. Mom continues to shiver dramatically, her face pulled long to impart terrible suffering.

Want your slippers?

It's bloody freezing.

I can get them for you.

I'll be fine.

Mom stares blankly into the distance. The valley shimmers green, whittled sharp by the heat, and birds sing from their branches without quite filling the silence, just as waves can beat a cliff for eons without breaking it.

He was better yesterday.

Mom, I don't wanna talk about it.

Well I do, and I will, because this is my house and

William's my son. I'll be damned if I listen to those frauds tell me he took his own life, when last I checked his heart's beating just fine, right there in his chest. The boy even looked at me yesterday.

Mom.

He looked me right in the eyes. I could tell he was there. Maybe he can't speak, but he's in there. He knew his mother was with him.

Mom.

He isn't going to hell, because he didn't do it. He got confused. But he didn't do it. Do you hear me? He's not in the ground, and as long as his heart is beating, I'm his mother, and you better get that into your head.

Ok, mom, I get it, now can we stop talking about it?

I'll stop talking about it when I bloody well please. You think I'm some sort of idiot? You think I'm out of my mind just because I don't believe he's gone?

Mom, the doctors told us. The blood flow was insufficient. There's no brain activity.

That's enough. That's quite enough out of you. You think I forgot, don't you? You think I can't remember what you did, Abilena?

What are you talking about?

Her eyes dart back and forth from the doorway to something just past my shoulder. She whispers.

You killed a child. And god cannot forgive you if you don't ask him to. And if you don't come to church and confess, you know damn well where you're going.

I look at her face in silence. It rises and bulges red with anger, softens into a pink limbo, and sags into white desperation. The sun's high now, oily and breathless in the unforgiving blue.

La Trinidad (Age 25)

There's a tube feeding Bill's arm, cause he's a flower kept in water. Come to the hospital every week to visit his body, this grave, and speak to it.

I'm pretty happy, Bill. Life's alright. Dad's been drinking less. I think he's met someone. I don't know. Don't really wanna know. But he's got a strange happiness about him. I know you fucking hated him. Or that's what you always told me. But somehow we're all tied together, right?

And Connie's happier. You'd have liked her, Billy. She's out now. In these horrible relationships, but at least she's out and seems happy. She dates awful girls.

I've been listening to music too. Lots and lots of Bowie. You always tried to tell me about him and now I'm listening to your favorite album. It cracks me up. Hunky Dory. Cause you were so rarely happy. You goddamn moron. Why'd you do it.

Mom's still waiting for you to come back. Keeps saying you didn't kill yourself, cause if you did you're going to hell, and blah blah blah. She's waiting for you to rise again like Jesus. Keeps saying god kept you here for a purpose. But he didn't. We did. We rushed you to the hospital. They plugged you into this nightmare. And now what? It was all bullshit, Billy. You were just sick. And you never got help. And now you're a drooling idiot. So fuck you. There's nothing to explain. It's pretty simple really. You're just an asshole. And I'm sorry I never got you help. I'm sorry I never understood what you were trying to say til you were done saying it. But I was just a fucking kid, Billy.

I tried going crabbing a couple weeks ago. Was real lonely. They weren't even moving. So I walked up to one and got on my knees to look at it. Still didn't move. So I put my finger on it. Nothing. So I picked it up and it was light as a feather. Cause there was nothing in there. Something happened to the crabs, Bill. So I gathered all the empty shells I could find, brought them into the studio, and built a court worthy of its king. Even had them smelt a silver crown. They're saying it's one of my best pieces, but I don't wanna sell it. I don't really know what to do with it. Hurts like a motherfucker. I guess the museum'll take care of that. Make it safe again. Frame it nice.

Oh fuck, that reminds me, Billy. Rodrigo never came down from the acid. It's so fucking weird. When he got home he took a second tab alone, the idiot. Tripped hard for three days. Tripped at the dinner table with his family. Tripped through football games. Then he sorta came down but his eyes stayed weird and he started talking about the law of threes. The father, the son, and the holy ghost. Won't stop talking about them. And eventually everybody stopped hanging out with him, cause he was creeping them out. But I stuck around. Cause sometimes in the morning he's fine for a bit. We'd have breakfast and he'd just seem a little agitated. Nothing too bad. But by midday he'd be babbling again. You know, Abi, everything comes in threes. So I ask him. What about eyes, Rodrigo? What about ears and arms and hands and legs and feet? Everything comes in threes. Everything. So I just stopped arguing with him. It's better that way. Yeah, Rodrigo, everything comes in threes.

Then I didn't see him for a long time. I mean like a few months, Billy. And the other day, out of nowhere, he shows up at our door. It's pretty late, like three in the morning on a Tuesday. And he's dressed in an Arabic robe. A djellaba. But it's all stained round the bottom, like he's been walking through mud. There's bits of leaves in his hair and he looks real happy and much older. Like he aged a decade. And he's showing me these three flowers. Must've stolen them from a rose garden. But they're all beat up. One of them's red, and two of them are white. And he just smiles at me without saying anything. So I say. Hi Rodrigo, you alright? And he just smiles some more. So I wait a bit, getting ready to close the door cause he's scaring me. But then he says. That's you. And I'm not sure what he's talking about, so I say. What's me? And he looks at me sorta sad. The red one, he says. So I say. Who are the other two? And he looks at me real sad like he's disappointed I'm so dumb. And he says. *El padre y el hijo.* The father and the son. That really fucked me up. I didn't know what to do. So I took the flowers. I knew he was saying goodbye but I didn't know what to do. Cause he was just standing there. So I invited him in. But he said no thanks. And I was relieved, to be honest. Didn't know what to do with him. So I hugged him and he smelled of dirt and sweat and cut grass. But I didn't wanna let go cause I didn't know if I'd see him again. And his breathing was so regular. He was so calm.

And I realized it would be fine. That sometimes you just have to say goodbye. So I let go. And he walked off. Just disappeared into the night.

Fuck, Billy. I really cried after that. And I put the flowers in the trash. Couldn't look at them. But I started wondering. What about mom, Billy? Why weren't there four roses? I know it's stupid, but I can't stop wondering about it. They come in threes. They come in threes. That fucking idiot. They found his robe in the trees near his house and he was gone for three weeks til the cops almost shot him for wandering naked in the *ávila*. They called his sister and she came to pick him up. Told her she needed to put him in a hospital. Thank god he didn't attack them, cause they woulda shot him. You know the cops. They beat him up pretty bad cause he wouldn't give them his name. So they just kept smacking him til he finally gave them his sister's number.

I came to visit him at her house right before they took him away to the hospital. He wouldn't say anything to me. Just smiled. Sister kept complaining that he wouldn't keep his clothes on. She'd dress him up and he'd just tear everything off and wander into the backyard and sit in a tree. Wouldn't speak to anyone. Always smiling though. And now he's in the hospital. I haven't visited him yet. Hope he's still smiling. I don't even know why I'm telling you this. Maybe cause you took so many drugs. And this is just another stupid drug story. Somebody took too much and lost their mind. Still, I can't shake the flowers. Keep thinking about them. Three flowers. But what happened to the fourth, Billy?

II

Sarah

He always has His reasons. In my dream God descended from the heavens to find me on the operating table, and from the discarded meat of my bosom his white hands sculpted two flawless children, as beautiful as William and Abilena but entirely incorruptible.

I can't wait to share this illumination with Pastor Jimenez. He always listens so intently, head cocked, with a piercing gaze that strips me down to my bare sins in the long flat beige hall with the small alcoves, each statuette afforded its own spotlight, each smiling, flanked on the shadowless walls by four black speakers, one for each dim corner, where the spiders hatch eggs directly beneath God's own eyes.

Whenever Pastor Jimenez's voice booms across the room, my eyes cross and a creeping dizziness begins in my toes and climbs my stockings beyond the legs. They still ache, these phantom breasts, with His love as old as earth itself, and so I steady myself by staring at the silver cross, tall, thin, with its double beam of yellow light casting geometry into the spidering shadows.

I think of him as I pin my hair up in a bun, the smell of Daniel's breath still poisoning my nostrils, a musky, animal odor coming from the bedroom as I choose the golden brooch in the bathroom mirror on Church Sunday, the one with all the stones, a colorful bird with red eyes, which the Pastor appreciates above all others.

My chest protects me from Daniel's violence. Go ahead, I told him. Go ahead and hit me, destroy me if you must, if that's what you were put here to accomplish. But he could not. He looked at me in terror, witness to His judgment, and never lifted a hand beyond that day. Perhaps a breastless woman is no woman. Perhaps there's no sport in her beating.

The brooch straightened, I think back to my conversation with the Pastor. You must never leave him, Sarah. You must stand by your husbands. Remember your vows. I promise to be true to you in good times and in bad, in sickness and in health. I will love you and honor you all the days of my life. Just as Jesus carried his cross, you must carry yours. I know these imperatives, Pastor, but what if he lays a hand upon my daughter? The lord tries us as He sees fit. Assuredly, a man will be judged according to his own sins, but these should not diminish the sanctity of your vows. And there are ways to turn a man towards God before the final judgment, especially a drinking man. Do you know of them, Sarah? Yes Pastor, and Lord knows I've tried, but he simply refuses to listen. He spits on God. He's told me this in no uncertain terms. Then let no one take away what the Lord has given you, Sarah, for your trials turn you all the more towards the light. God never gives us more than we can carry, but he does not mean for us to carry it alone. Sometimes we must find strength in his glory. Do not weep, Sarah. I cannot help it. Then weep, but do not despair. Weep with joy at the knowledge of your certain deliverance.

So I wept in the confessional, and through the diamonds of light I could see his neatly trimmed beard. The way the Pastor smells of pastry and cream. Certainly he must know. Poor Sarah. Her confessions are always the same. The confessions of a weak woman. Despite which Pastor Jimenez gives me strength. With every sermon. With every look he says: you are the most devoted. You are the chestless steeple of our flock. With his soft wooden eyes. The lord has great plans for a woman of your caliber. Do not waver.

His words provide me strength as I apply discrete lipstick, some light foundation, and a touch of mascara. I finger my prosthesis into position, the straps digging painfully into my body. I notice a flaw in the carved wood of the mirror as I brush my teeth for three minutes and step into my heels. There are no holes in my stockings so I take a pill for the headache and hold my nose as I step lightly through the bedroom, past the poison that sleeps, and close the door soundlessly behind me.

Abilena's sitting at the top of the stairs in that white tank top and those jeans. Not a grain of makeup and dressed like a man.

Good morning, Abilena.

Morning, mom.

Not painting?

Not yet. Haven't had my coffee.

I suppose there's no point asking if you'd like to join me?

Actually, I would.

Really?

Yeah.

Well I suppose there's a first time for everything. Go put on a dress.

Her eyes harden into a squint as the gears turn in Abilena's head. Then she smiles and answers me.

Ok, Mom.

And scampers down the stairs with all the mannerisms of a teenage boy. When she returns, she's wearing a navy blue cotton dress and looks almost like a real woman. Suddenly I feel like an old lady taking her daughter to church. I've been blessed with two wonderful children. If only William were here to walk with us! But nonetheless I enjoy Abilena's presence as we step out the front door and walk down the street, along the crumbling walls of other homes, over the cracked sidewalks and crushed fruit, hair caressed by the long drooping tree leaves.

Careful, Abi.

I saw it.

Might be embarassing to step in that.

Among the rotten stench of sweet flowers, mashed mangoes, and burning meat, I can feel William's presence in the morning air. My son, born after twenty three hours of labor. Nearly tearing me apart. But white and frail when he finally arrived. Barely pink at all. Not like Abilena, so red she nearly scared me to death. The doctors reassured me: there's nothing wrong with your daughter. Still I would look down into her crib and marvel at the redness of her skin and the roundness of her body. More of a corpuscle than a child. Until her angelic yellow hair began to grow and I could tell immediately. A mother often can. Abilena would be the beautiful one.

Daniel

In the nightmare, Javier is cutting strips of flesh from the peacock bass and placing em side by side on the long wooden table. He's bloated and dead, blue and white and purple, puffed out like a fucking sea cucumber. And the strips're just thick sheets of slimy scale, shiny and wet with their black and yellow rings.

Javier, how did you get to be so good with the knife?

Dunno, boss. You pleased?

Yes. It's good work. You're a good man and a good fisherman. Except for the drinking.

Can't help the drinking, *jefe*.

And Javier keeps whittling away at the fish. Whittling and sweating.

You're gonna be dead a long fucking time Javier, and there's nobody left to provide for your family.

Won't you, boss?

Javier's got no eyeballs in his head, just two black holes where they used to be. Behind him in buckets they're piled, whole naked fish, pink and stripped of their flesh and tossed in heaps.

Won't you, boss?

I wake up sweating in the sheets. Sarah's asleep next to me and I'm thirstier n'hell. The water makes my body ache and I take a swig of rum to help smooth everything out. Lie down again and soon the pain settles into a flat noise. Sink back into sleep but it don't feel right. Cause when I was a kid I saw something like.

Pink puppies in a flour sack.

Listen to me, danny. You listen careful.

So I do, I listen real careful to Papa, his thick jaw with the shaving cuts and smelling of firewood.

You hear them noises?

They're screaming, Papa.

Yes they are, you little dummy. I ain't scared about the screams, danny. I'm scared you don't know what's making em. You think it's puppies, don't you?

Yes, papa.

Well they ain't. They're just a shame and they never shoulda happened in the first place.

Don't answer Papa, but I think those puppies can't breathe all pushed together in the flour sack.

Stop lookin at the sack, danny. Stop it. They were never

born. How many times we gotta go through this with you. They're altricial. You know what that means, you little dummy?

They can't see or hear, Papa.

That's right. They're not even born yet. Nothin more than rats. And you know what we do to rats. What do we do to rats, danny?

Kill em, Papa.

So that's what I'm gonna need you to do. Take care of em. Look at me. Don't you start cryin. Don't you start. I'll give you somethin to be sad about if you start cryin. You're gonna take the sack and bring it down to the pond and drop some rocks in there. Then you're gonna throw it into the middle of the pond. Not the sides with the mud and the reeds. The middle where the water is. You hear me?

Yes papa.

Then you come on up for dinner, cause your mama ain't gonna wait forever. She mad already. Go on, son. Be a man. I'll be up here takin care we got wood for tomorrow mornin.

So little Daniel makes his way down the hill in his rubber boots and osh kosh shortalls, sticking his fingers in and out of his nose and dragging the squirming sack behind him towards the pond.

I'm dreaming. Another fucking rum nightmare. Can even hear Sarah preparing for church behind the sound of the puppies

My skull's a sickly pounding mess like never again

Just a few nips

Falling, falling

Danny's walking down the hill. I know what comes next and I don't wanna

So I think about the standing and the aspirin and the first drink and the puking and

The hill's long and craggly and my feet chip at rocks as I stumble downslope. Keep my head straight so Papa can't see I'm crying. Then I'm round the bend and he can't see me no more. Make a sound louder than the puppies then, crying like a little spoiled baby. Not a baby boy. I'm a Man! Papa's son. So I set the sack on the edge of the pond where the mud's hard. Find a couple rocks. Rough edges gonna crush the rats. Specially their eyelids glued shut with black and gooey. So I put all the rocks on the ground next to the sack and look at it hard, the straw rough and shifting, making those worse sounds. Then I untie the sack and pick the biggest rock, holding it above the dark. But I can't look down so instead I look up and see the big pink sky with the black blue top where the sun can't reach. Trees all over. Fields all over. Spiders dancing on the pond water. Muddy bottom water. Nobody around.

The puppies keep crawling til the bag flops over and they start coming out. Nothing but baby dogs, and some with their eyes already open. I hold the rock above my head cause my arms are tired, and I just watch em crawl for a while.

I could keep em in my room. I could keep em under the bed if I just get em to shut up.

Keep quiet down there.

Idiot, puppies can't learn to be quiet. And what about feeding em? I'm hungry. I can't give em no part of my part. So I watch em crawling til they get to the muddy water and start sinking a bit. One of em does. Then others are barking too. I can see em hurting in their half death, breathing horrible mud, choking and barking like little babies. One of em already close to dead in the reeds. And my chest's gonna explode with horrible crying cause I can't breathe. There's so much mud everywhere on my boots. To take care of em all. Pushing down into the mud with my rubber boots to make sure nothing's moving in the mud down there. Until none of em are moving anymore. Then I fish into the mud with my fingers for the squashed little babies and throw em into the sack with the rocks and toss em all into the middle of the pond where they disappear into the brown water.

Wonder if the fish're gonna eat em. A big fish could

eat the whole sack. We put a goldfish in there once and now there's half-red-half-white fish. Half-red-half-black fish. Wash my hands in the water but there's too much mud. Wash my face in the water to hide my crying. Then I walk around the bend and up the hill. Back home. The door makes a puppy sound as it's opening. Papa's sitting by the lamp. Mama's angry.

You got mud everywhere! Your face and your overalls. Look at your boots. What are we gonna do with you?

And Papa just sits and eats and doesn't talk. So Mama rubs my face and sits me down at the table and I look across at Papa. He's eating like a Man and I'm a Man. He's got a mean eye, like he knows what I done. Rotten puppies'll get me whipped. But I sit strong on the hard wooden chair and reach for some meat. I'll never tell. I'll never let him whip the boy in my nightmare.

I was nothing but a little boy. Won't wake if I can help it, not from this nightmare, not from any nightmare. Cause when I'm awake all I can see is that dead boy Billy sitting bony and ferocious. Cornered animal won't let me drink in peace. Had a Papa, then was a Man, then was Bill's Dad, then

Now I'm Bill's dead

That night we had a conversation in his bedroom. With Sarah and Abilena in the tv room. He looked at me angrier than hell.

You've never told me once. You've never told me once.

It's not true, Bill. I've said it. It's not easy for me, but you're my son and I do love you.

That's when he swung at me

Shattering headache in strong beating hammers. Skull pushed into the rims. Reach under the bed for rum and take a swig. Stand up and get to the bathroom in time. Then I take another swig. This one stays down. Splash some water on my face. She's gone to church to see that Pastor.

Once I'm steady I won't drink today, sore need for some time off. Gonna drive to see her lips and mouth smoking casually on the balcony. Kid's always playing on the rug. Maria Rita. That's where I gotta be. Fuck the rest. Kiss me a little longer, Maria Rita. Never think about Billy when I'm around her. Piss longer than a man's ever. Take a couple more swigs and shower long and hot, but the water can't reach me. Brush my teeth. Mouth wash. Tap a pack of cigarettes and light one on the balcony. The valley's still green. The *ávila* stands. The sky hasn't fallen. The order of things continues for another cycle. Til it doesn't.

My son's a vegetable and my wife's praying to that fucking pussy. But today I take the car to see Maria Rita and leave the rest to the goddamn birds. Cause there's nothing like that woman to stop all the fucking thinking.

Sarah

Two yellow finches. They circle above the entrance as the Pastor greets Hilda and the twins on the church steps, cutting a sharp figure in his cream suit and freshly pressed yellow shirt. The birds dart through the bell tower and settle in the branches of the *guarumbo* with its thick green hands splayed against the whitewashed church facade. Pastor Jimenez always wears the same brown shoes, modest and reassuring. He touches the top of each boy's head with the flat of his palm, benevolent, with the same unassuming dignity he uses to hold their grandmother's shriveled hands.

Hilda stares at him in adoration before slowly making her way into the church. She'll take a seat in the front pew as always, with those boys never sitting still. Nobody can fault the old widow of course, even though someone should tell her: boys require a firm hand. All boys do. If nature were free to take its own course they would all grow beastly ill, thin and white with savage eyes, more like animals than men. Yes, it takes a firm hand to forge a gentleman.

Good morning, Sarah.

Good morning, Pastor.

Two hands, one above, one below, neither warm nor cold. He smiles at me and nods to Abi.

And this must be.

Yes, of course, excuse me Pastor. You haven't met my daughter yet. She usually attends another church. This is Abilena. Abi, meet Pastor Jimenez.

Alfredo

Abilena. Her name is Abilena, splitting the blue sky with her simple name. I cannot touch her hands for fear they will burn me. Burning, my God, and burning, God. The long calves from beneath her blue dress. I summon every ounce of strength to steady my eyes and meet her gaze for even a fleeting second, God, please steady my gaze.

Bienvenida, señorita.

I am young again in her presence and I can taste cigarettes even though I haven't smoked in years. My innards are burning. Desire so unfamiliar, flooding through me as I meet Sarah's daughter. I'm completely unable to speak and they seem to take my silence as a cue to enter the church, leaving me to deal with the rest of the gathering crowd. I say nothing out of sorts. If the body could speak it would seldom deliver sermons. My words are fraudulent, but my body says: welcome to the stomach of blood, rib of heart, rib of burning to sit.

Hola Pastor, says a member of my flock as I sit hard on the stone steps.

Hola, I answer.

Is everything alright, *Pastor*?

Yes, thank you. Just a little dizzy.

My penis is pushing at the stiff cloth of my pant leg. Burning dimly from some earthen netherworld, a hot, rising, unholy wave. Now I'm completely sitting on the stairs and I observe only their shoes as they walk into the church, baffled at my behavior. A brown loafer. White heels with a skin-colored bandage. Skin burning. I close my eyes and summon images of filth in an attempt to quell the fire in my belly. Shit, shit, shit. Push a shit from the earth with old ladies thick and hot, never before. Push a horrible shit. Dead cockroaches. Frozen ice cream, too hard to eat. Frozen meat. By the grace of God my erection lessens and the heat in my belly dissipates, leaving behind a vague sense of confusion and unease. They're waiting for me in the pews and I stand, straighten my pants, and walk up the stairs with a posture worthy of the Lord's home.

I walk calmly down the aisle, past Abilena in the third row, beside Sarah with her daughter Abilena, as if nightfall were of no particular importance, for sin to exist so plainly in the daylight! Eyes trained on their Pastor, they await His words. The congregation of men and women. But in the light of day! Like a young boy again. I lean into the dusty black microphone bending from the wooden pulpit and begin reading from yesterday's notes.

The sermon goes the usual way. Thrice they rise. Thrice they sit. Two psalms. She keeps squinting at the photocopied program to discern when this charade will end. Abilena can see right through the shabby pastor and places not a penny in the basket. There are no pockets in her dress.

Once the service is over, everyone files patiently into the foyer while I stay behind, waiting for the last of them to disappear. I find myself short of breath and wheezing as I take a seat in the forgiving penumbra of the confessional booth. Lord, grant me relief. The sound of a wooden box creaking within an empty room as I bring myself to the unfortunate in a handkerchief, pants gathered around my ankles. My come smells like old water in a vase or ripe cherry blossoms in the spring. A vegetal rot. I fold it neatly into the handkerchief and discard the unfortunate consequence of my capricious body.

The fever having passed, I feel like myself once more. Still I wait two whole minutes before pushing the brass knobs, once more at peace among my congregation after the wooden doors part to reveal a good-natured crowd of Christian men and women.

Abilena

Even the cookies taste like dust if it were wet and old. Liver spots on their hands and sweet faces turned to him, like he knows a goddamn thing. For mom he's Harrison Ford stepped right out of the television, but the pastor knows I don't belong here and never makes eye contact with me, the scaredy cat. But I'm gonna have to do it no matter what. Cause I'm not gonna sit through another one of those sermons in that awful beige nightmare from the seventies. And all the standing. Goes right up into my skull like a dry wind. Worn dry carpet and not even beautiful. Isn't the whole point to stand in awe? Of this man? Of this building? So they mutter round the plastic tables and nibble over paper plates. Mom I'm gonna rid you. I'm gonna take care of what's been eating you. Cause if you listen to this man, then I'll talk to this man. Maybe he can get through. I certainly hope so. Cause you need to face reality. Bill's fucking dead.

Mister Jimenez. Mister.

I touch his elbow and he draws away, dumbstruck. Mom intervenes to protect the holy man's dignity.

It's pastor, Abi. Pastor Jimenez.

But his face softens into an idiotic smile.

Yes my child, what can I do for you?

Could I speak with you in private?

Abi, please don't bother the pastor. If you want to ask him something, do it now. Otherwise just enjoy the tea.

She looks to him for approval.

No bother at all, Sarah, it would be my pleasure to listen to whatever your daughter has to say.

His soft voice strikes her like a whip and she shrinks a little but stays close, hard eyes on me.

Well, what is it, ah, Abilena?

I.

Don't be embarrassed, my child.

It's about mother.

What about me?

She can't accept what happened to Bill.

Nothing happened to William.

You mean your brother, the young man who's in a coma?

Is that what she told you?

That's the truth, Abi.

No it's not. Bill's not in a coma. Bill's got no brain activity. The doctors say he's never gonna come back, cause the damage is permanent.

Abilena! What do you think you're doing? Pastor, I apologize. Please don't listen to her.

He looks at me with his pretty brown eyes and long black lashes.

Does your mother's faith disturb you, Abilena?

Her faith in what, pastor?

Mom's trying to pull him away but he holds his ground.

Her faith in god.

Abi, we need to leave.

No. I'm not gonna leave. She listens to you, pastor. Please help her see the truth. I want my mom back.

But she's shaking red and holding her breath. And the pastor speaks calmly.

Perhaps the doctors are right.

They're not, pastor! Don't listen to her nonsense!

Old ladies turn from their cookies to stare at mom. But through his fear, the pastor continues.

Well even if they are. Your mother still has a right to her faith.

Sarah

My husband shot me full of rotten seed and I gave birth to two serpents. To slither like this into the last place I have left! To speak to the Pastor as if he were nothing but a man! With her birth the Lord punished me for my weakness. Would that I could strangle her in the womb.

And to watch him respond with such calm and compassion, when she deserves nothing. This man. His calm. His everlasting calm. I have a right to my faith. Nothing you can steal. Those are His words, you little cunt. I should have known better, bringing you here to poison this congregation.

Let William be dead then, let him linger in that half place. There is no William, only another snake in the pit. Finally I summon the wherewithal to speak.

You will leave now, Abilena.

Alright.

You will get out of this place and never return.

I'll see you at home, Mom.

Like Hell you will.

Abilena

Two finches in light orange plumage. They observe me sitting on the church stairs, and when I close my eyes I see the outline of mom's face torn into a snarl. The birds seem made of wax on the long thin trump of the pumpwood tree, bending awkwardly into a dense burst of green.

I think of Mother when she was younger, when she'd let her ponytail down into a gentle spread of blonde, like a lioness with a lion's coif. A real woman. Not a lady. She'd lie in her one-piece on the lawn chair over the crabgrass and I'd crawl her feet as she sipped mashed fruit and liquor.

Let me paint them purple, Mom?

Oh alright, dear.

So I'd close one eye and hold my breath, the grass a sweltering blur as I concentrated on one perfect toe. Dad would wear turquoise bathing shorts to labor in the garden, brown and sweaty with raybans, cigarette hanging from his lips, grunting mid-song, muscles jammed, pushing at a spade or stretched into clippers. Cause it was good for a while. Til the weekends curled in the sun and burnt to black excrement. Til she kept her ponytail up and he stopped singing and the garden grew tangled and ugly. They'd yell downstairs and the chairs would scrape the kitchen floor til she went to bed and he stood in the doorway of our bedroom singing *La Bamba* with a drink in his hand while Billy slept and I faked it. And I also remember the dinner table scene, with mom trying to sound hopeful.

Isn't it nice that dad quit smoking? Isn't it nice? Your father smells much better now.

And he'd smile grimly and sip the whiskey. She'd never dare touch his whiskey. Then he started coming home later. Til one night she woke us up saying

William. William. Get up. You get up this instant. I need your help with something. Your father claims he hasn't been smoking. Claims he hasn't touched a cigarette in weeks. Get up, William, for god's sake.

Bill got out of bed and I could see his tiny white chest in the darkness, all bones and breath and pajama bottoms. And the back of his head with the jumping cow-lick. Then she pushed him forward into the obscurity of dad's paunch.

Smell your father.

What?

Smell your father, William. Then you tell me. You tell me if he hasn't smoked. Go on. Smell him.

And Bill's fingers crushed into small trembling fists. As he stepped forward. And sniffed like a cartoon would. Real loud and exaggerated.

No, he said, in a congealed falsetto.

What do you mean, no?

He doesn't smell like nothing, just dad.

And that's when dad smacked Bill real hard on the side of the head.

Don't you lie to your mother, you little shit. Don't you fucking lie to your mother.

So mom lost her cool and started screaming.

Get out! You get out of this room immediately! Touch my child! You worthless liar!

And they continued to make noise from the kitchen til they stopped. And Bill climbed into bed and never talked about it again. But I can still remember her voice saying it.

Smell your father. Go on.

So I open my eyes and rise from the church stairs to see the birds are gone. Everybody's still inside the building, so I walk home alone, down the streets with walls on both sides and the quintas with their painted tile, iron gates and barbed wire. But my thoughts are so loud I can't see the trees or listen to the birds. Just my head buzzing with the Pastor's words.

Your mother has a right to her faith.

And mom's words.

Like hell you will.

And Bill's words.

Don't let them kill you. You gotta stay alive despite mom and dad.

And how he's never gonna say more words for me to remember.

When I arrive home, dad's off to see his lover. I can tell because he always washes the car before. Now he's fumbling with the keys and glances up at me, hair sorta slicked in a skeleton puff.

Have fun, dad.

So he looks at me sideways from his rolled down window.

I said have fun, dad.

But he drives off in a sputter. So I open the front door, walk into the kitchen, and pour some water into the stockpot. Stare at the blue rim diffusing into wisps of purple iridescence til the tea is brewed and I sit on the torn leather stool in the art studio. But it's impossible to paint. Nothing happening but words chasing circles. Cause the stupid brush won't paint a goddamn thing. Til finally I stand up and walk into the kitchen and pick up the phone and dial Connie's boutique.

I need your help.

Are you alright?

I need your help, Cons.

With what?

They're awful.

Who?

All of them. The whole family.

I know.

They're just the fucking worst.

I know, *flaca*. Come by the boutique. I'll get Maribel to cover for me so I can take the day off. She owes me one.

Really?

Of course.

You're a fucking champion.

You kidding me, skinny? Sounds like a great time. Finally you're the moody bitch.

You smelly old cunt. You better watch your back.

Sarah

The faint smell of moth wings in his sturdy arms, away from the prying eyes of those gossiping hags. My tears stain the lapel of his cream suit, aged in the closet of a solitary man, a Man of God.

Sarah, you must cease crying, I keep telling myself. You simply must. But I can't for fear that he'll release his grip, forcing me to face again the dull silence of total loss. Was it not Jesus who said. If anyone comes to me and does not hate her own husband and children, yes, and even her own life, she cannot be my disciple. Whoever does not bear her own cross and follow me cannot be my disciple. So therefore, any one of you who does not renounce all that she has cannot be my disciple.

Are you alright, Sarah?

I'm lost, Pastor. My husband. Rotten. My children. One dead. The other a stranger. I can't continue.

This isn't the end of your journey, Sarah. The realm of God is opening its doors to you, and you're finally ready to enter it. The gift of desperation is yours. The material world is crumbling around you. Scales are falling from your eyes so you can better see His kingdom.

Well then where do I go next, Pastor? I don't know what to do. Help me.

Alfredo steps away from me, staring into my eyes, then

leans in and slips the wedding band from my ring finger. He must feel my heart pounding through every bone in my body.

Daniel

Almost pound down the flimsy door. Kid crying somewhere in there. Asshole tighter than a dock ring. Dick harder than rock. Peephole dark and light as she checks for danger.

Open up.

Cálmate hombre. Calm down.

Cracks the door, chain taut so I can see her body fleshed out in shades of olive, two small bruises beneath her right knee. The smell of legs oiled to dull bronze.

Let me in.

Cálmate. Have some patience.

I'll kill you.

You'll do nothing til I let you.

I'll break this fucking door down.

Pubic hair like charcoal vines climbing her lower belly, mixed up with the scars. Way her hair falls twirling, snagged on cold sharp nipples, baring her teeth like a cornered bitch. And the wailing of her pup from the rug.

Please.

The scar on her arm from the childhood injection in some crumby hospital. Fine black hair on her upper-lip and those dark drooping green eyes, tired of the world's endless hard-on.

Maybe. Only if you beg.

I'll bust the door to woodchips.

My threats don't even register with this woman. She looks at me with absolute certainty.

You won't. You'll get on your fucking knees and beg.

I undo my belt, pull down my fly, and push my prick through the crack in the door. She leans forward, just a mass of black hair hovering inches from my face. Then a long drip of saliva stretches slowly from her lips like tree sap. A cool shiver as it makes contact.

Touch it. Please touch it, Maria Rita.

Then beg me, you fucking faggot.

So I get on my knees, underwear caught beneath my balls.

Please.

Door slams but I pull back in time. The slow grind of rusted metal and silence. I look down at the ugly gleam of her spit on my red flesh. Then I reach for the doorknob and turn it slowly, expecting a cruel trick, but the door slides open effortlessly, oiled to reveal her shape, legs wide on the sofa, mouth fierce in defiance, pulling herself apart from across the room, cunt pink and swollen between the dust-caked soles of her feet. My blood-jammed skull plodding me forward til I wrap my hand around her throat. She makes sounds like an animal or child. The pain ceases as I finally find it, the sliding collapse of everything I know, funneled into this woman, this tarpit. The child is silent now, sitting on the rug with indifferent eyes trained on our convulsions.

Baby, baby, baby, baby, baby, baby. Oh my fucking god.

The steaming gurgle of caving soil.

Ma. Maria. Maria Rita.

Come inside me, Danny. Just fucking come inside me.

Then my skull lifted through skin, floating up, up, up, crushed into the burning ring of a long-dead sun. God is Maria Rita's cunt.

Sarah

Alfredo drops the ring into my unzipped purse and allows me to sit on the leather bench as he washes his hands in hot water. White steam drifts in the candlelight.

This city won't do. You'll need a peaceful place for your body and mind to heal.

He's pale as he faces the mirror, eyes steady and wooden. I look down at the crude birds woven into his Persian carpet, their dark plumage interrupted by a coarse ladder of red and white feathers. The hunter gripping his bow. A blood-red knit.

I can never be whole.

Please Sarah. Cast aside your aspersions. They won't do you any good.

I begin unbuttoning my blouse.

What are you doing, Sarah?

Showing you.

I unhook the bra and let the prosthesis fall from me. Alfredo doesn't flinch, his hands frozen in the dim light having never reached the towel.

Now can you see, Pastor? There won't be any

remembering. The past is lost forever.

Each drop of water disturbs the silence of the Pastor's inner chambers as it falls from his fingers. My eyes can see everything at once. His wooden desk cut from rough wood. An old-fashioned plume. An immodest baroque chair. The cheap yellow cloth of his sleeves rolled to the elbow and the slight breeze against the savaged skin of my barren chest.

Sister... I didn't know.

And now you do. I'll never feed a child again. My husband won't touch me. There's nothing left.

Alfredo opens a drawer and produces a red blanket lined with cheap velvet.

Cover yourself or you'll catch cold.

But I don't reach for his outstretched hand. Rather I stand naked without shame.

Look at me, Alfredo.

Then, turning slowly, he lets the blanket fall to the floor, wearily settling into his chair.

Get out of here, he says.

Daniel

Come trickles her inner-thighs as she carries the baby to the metal-rimmed formica table. I smoke a cigarette and watch her remove the runt's diaper and wipe shit from its rash-covered asshole. Cool breeze from the setting sun.

Can't see the daylight through the thick canopy of her cunt. Each breath her cunt. Each drop of spit. Two weeks before it fades. Taste it on every cigarette. In every drink. Infects everything. Nothing outruns Maria Rita's cunt. I put the cigarette in a dixie cup. Crackles as the water extinguishes it. She's barely said a fucking word. Not like Sarah who spoke and spoke. Had to tell her one time. Why'd you always need to talk? I don't know, she said. And she really didn't. Nor do I. Even less when I'm here. Watching Maria Rita change the kid, come-slicked hair blackening her thighs. Other day the bitch asks me.

You ever been to war?

Hesitated. In the end I couldn't lie to Maria Rita. Something felt wrong about it.

No, I never went to war.

How d'you get out of it?

Didn't give them my new address.

And they couldn't find you?

Didn't come looking. Then Carter pardoned all the draft dodgers in seventy-seven. Better things to do I guess. Than chase an old man.

But you weren't old then.

I was stupid then. Young. But Billy and Abilena were born and I knew enough to tell Vietnam wasn't a fucking hunting trip. I thought my kid deserved a dad. Cause I'd seen some of the guys come back already. So I stayed in South America. Dumb little shit. Didn't know my ass from my elbow.

You're still little.

Am I?

She stares at me, green eyes like a wet jungle pit.

How bout now?

Less.

How bout now?

Even lesser.

You really are a little whore.

I am not just a whore. I will be your whore or no whore.

Then you can be my whore.

Do you love me, *papi?*

Fuck love. Look what you're doing to me. Touch it, Maria Rita. You feel that? No lie. This apartment's the only place I can tell the truth.

Then tell me the truth, Danny. But tell me the truth a little rougher this time. I like it when you make me suffer a little.

Just a little?

Just enough.

William

Can't speak, can't move, can't even blink. I was left behind to watch my body slowly disintegrate, and sure as shit, that's what's happening. A ring of negative space is expanding in the middle of my field of vision, surrounded by an irreversible yellow light, the kind that stays behind when you stare too long at the sun. I'm pretty sure that's permanent damage (in the doctor's words).

Isabel, my nurse, (wish she would suck my prick cause she sounds exactly like this girl I used to know, who would never touch a deformed freak like me) pulls my eyelids open in the morning and closes them every night so I can rest my eyes. The doctors told her not to bother cause I'm dead meat anyway, but she believes the light will somehow reach me, even if I'm a vegetable. Thank fuck for that, cause it's boring in the dark. I haven't been able to feel my toes for the last couple of weeks. The numbness is gaining ground.

Abi and Connie are in the room with me. (The dream I had last night involved fucking *pequeña*, but my prick was limp and I pissed inside her instead, it was warm and, I don't want to think about this, why am I thinking about this, focus on what's around me so it stops, stop stop stop)

I can only make out their features if they're standing near, cause in the distance everything fades to grey. Even the posters on the walls have become illegible, floating in a cottony mist.

Sexually transmitted diseases you catch from every person because our entire generation is riddled with them. The proper way to wash your hands for hours until you scrub your skin off. Influenza. Bullshit cartoon characters smiling and hugging.

Abilena leans over to kiss my forehead and for a moment I'm lost in her blonde hair and everything's golden and I can smell that she's happy. She doesn't need anything from me cause I'm not her older brother anymore. Sweat is trickling from my armpits and soaking the bedding. (Not an erection though, please not an erection.) Then there's the constant itch of my ass pressed to itself and the thud, thud, thud of my beating heart and my internal organs palpitating and secreting ooze.

Abilena wipes the side of my mouth with a napkin. I want to tell her don't bother, I'm gonna keep drooling indefinitely now. That's where I'm heading. Slowly to a slug's death.

Hi Bill. Connie came to see you again.

Do you like my tits today, Bill?

(I do, Connie. I'd like to paint them with cooking oil and fuck them.)

You were right about the parents.

(I know.)

Wish you could hear me say it.

(I can.)

They're nuts.

(You'll be fine. I love you so much and wish I could tell you.)

I don't know what to do anymore.

(Just leave.)

Mom's done with the food but she's god-crazy. I think she's in love with her pastor. And dad's got a lover too. I miss you, Bill.

(I know you do. I fucked up. I fucked everything up.)

Abi cries for a few minutes and Connie comforts her. Then Connie leans over me and I can smell her perfume.

I miss you too, Bill, even though I never met you. I love the silent types. I'd suck your cock if you were still alive.

(Fuck.)

Abi laughs.

You're awful, Connie.

After they kiss me goodbye, Isabel appears in the doorway.

Hello, Willy.

(Don't call me that.)

Your sister seems lovely. Did you enjoy her visit? You look happy. You don't smell so good though.

(That's because I shat myself as they left.)

Maybe we need to clean you up some.

(Yes we do.)

I can see her fingers stretching the blue latex. The glove makes a satisfying snap. Then she gently tilts my body to the side. (Don't let me fall over. The fucking feeding tube would mangle my guts.) But Isabel's always careful and I don't have a choice, so I trust her and she removes the diaper. Same as usual since they installed the feeding tube: she gives me a slow dry wipe and then uses a moist cloth to circle my asshole. My legs feel like empty yogurt, weird pleasure shooting down all the paths the heroin used to take. Feels sort of like pissing after you come. I don't want her to stop.

(Don't stop, Isabel.)

After the first time she cleaned me, I started shitting

myself several times a day. She was too smart to fall for that, so as punishment she left me sitting in it for hours and I got a pretty bad rash. Now I stick to once a day.

See? Death isn't so bad.

Daniel

The fish are belly up, thousands of them. Blackwood pushing through the dead white lake, water shining as I walk down the dock.

How long?

Worst it's been, boss. Started about three weeks ago.

Carlos speaks slowly and carefully as he looks out over the patches of rot.

The smell's fucking horrible.

I cough and Carlos hands me a tube of menthol. I smear some on my upper lip and on the inside of my nostrils, then wipe my tears with a handkerchief. That's when Carlos really gets going.

Couldn't get a hold of you, *jefe*. We stopped three days ago. Most of the *gringos* wouldn't even get on the boats. Those who did wouldn't last the hour. Used to be some empty space between the fish. Now it's hard to cast at all. We kept the money like you said, but Camilo almost got shot yesterday. This drunk *gringo* had a rifle. He was pissed. I don't blame him, boss. These aren't fishable waters.

I see that, Carlos. How's your wife?

She's worried, boss.

The kids?

They're fine. Thanks for asking, *jefe*.

Did you see where the trucks went?

Beats me.

What did they look like?

Big and blue. With big red words on them.

What words?

I don't know.

What the fuck do you mean, you don't know?

Can't read.

They were too far away?

Can't read, boss.

Of course not. Goddamnit.

I'm sorry.

Nothing to be ashamed of, Carlos. You're a good fisherman. Did you see anybody?

No.

Ningún gringo?

Ningún.

I look at his face to make sure he isn't lying. Maybe they paid him off. I can never tell with these *morochos*, but he's probably telling the truth. Either way, there's nothing to be done.

Ok. Tell your family I said hi.

Thank you *jefe*, I will.

I begin walking back to land. Carlos stays staring off the end of the dock.

What are you gonna do about this, boss?

I don't know. And stop fucking calling me *jefe*.

Si, señor.

You can go home Carlos, I'll be in touch.

He looks at me kinda confused before he walks back to land, kickstarts his old Suzuki, and takes off in a cloud of dust, the ugly sound of his motorcycle getting smaller as I stare at the pink horizon. I walk to the edge of the dock again and dip two fingers in the water. Bring them to my mouth and instantly regret it.

Fuck.

I walk to the car and grab a dixie cup from the dashboard, toss the cigarette butts into the weeds, and walk back to the edge of the dock to dip the cup in the foul water. Then I sit behind the wheel with the windows closed, breathing the menthol in and out, looking at the poisonous rust-colored water.

Pendejos. They fucked my lake.

I can see the top of the cup, a red circle reflected on the inside of the windshield. Then I slam the steering wheel until my palms go numb and I turn the fucking key and rev the goddamn motor.

Abilena

Her lonely breasts sit folded on the dining room table. Mom left a note next to her prosthetics, but I can't bring myself to read it, so I walk into the kitchen and stare at the butter dish. There's enough butter for about five or six slices of toast, and mom left, maybe forever. Next to the butter is an unripe avocado, but you can fix that by slicing the avocado and cooking it in a pan. Goes brown and softens. Or just leave the slices in lemon for an hour. Plenty tricks really. Like chopping up fennel and laying it down in some olive oil with rock salt. Take the tang right out of it, make it right for salad. Or chop a red onion and lay him in a glass of water. Wait a few minutes. Five. Then drain it. Cause mom taught me that. Not cause she tried, but cause I asked. A lady doesn't ask so many questions, she always used to tell me. A lady.

Mom's note sits on the dining room table, ebbing stiffly in the breeze. The pulp of something that meant something. Words mean something. Cause we have what we say. And we have what we do. And we have what we take with us and what we find once we get there.

This whole house'll be gone. It's sinking into the lagoon. Each red heron carries a piece of furniture in his mouth, cleaning up the mess we made of this family. They take our stuff all the way to Bonaire and live in a giant nest made of ruined furniture. It's so big that every grandfather clock's just another twig in the pile. They've glued them all together with the ensanguined mash of dead flamingoes. This isn't a cleanup job, it's fucking murder.

So the furniture's not even here. I'm floating through empty space to reach mom's note, which I read quickly and then sit to cry. Even though they're old tears. Nothing new with mama. Just another part of saying goodbye. So everything's just hello and goodbye. And we don't choose either.

Stop. Just stop. Your name's Abilena and you're sitting in a house. Not a home. A reality. A concrete implacable unstoppable physical goddamn reality. Get a grip on yourself. Cause she finally left us. And Bill's gone too. Now there's only daddy. So I look up at the front door and he trods wearily through it wearing an old checkered flannel and his work jeans. Puts a dixie cup on the shelf. It's half-filled with red liquid and dad's looking about a million years old. He's getting tired.

Bibi.

Dad.

Come here.

And he holds me tight. For a second he seems like a normal Father. Then from the silence, my voice.

Mom's gone.

Words muffled to his chest. And the reverberation of

his answer.

The lake's dead.

Then silence again and we stand there til my legs get tired and his arms tremble. So we head to the garden where I climb the tree and he lies in the crabgrass til the moon comes up. Just me in the sky and dad on the ground. Then he says it, real quiet and steady like a prayer.

We need to get Bill.

Daniel

The hospital looks like a big grey egg carton. Never seen the place before. Guess all my accidents were outside Caracas. *Gringos* getting hurt mostly. Hook in the arm. Hook in the face. Losing a finger trying to cut a fish with a *machete*. Fainting from sunstroke. Stupid shit like that. I always drove them to a run-down little hospital near the lake where they took forever to help you, *gringo* or not. Then there was the time I hooked Bill's little white ass. I remember laughing so hard I couldn't pull the hook out. I fished my son! I fished my goddamn son. He didn't think it was funny. Never thought anything I did or said was funny. Sometimes you get so smart you can't see the humor in anything. Then you can't enjoy the good things in life, like a clean lake or a cigarette after a meal. No more whiskey for me, though. Once we get out the city there'll be no more whiskey. None to buy. None to drink. But I'll bring a couple cartons to smoke.

You ready, Dad?

Abilena seems feisty. I can tell she's gonna be leading this operation, on account of her enthusiasm and the fact that she's visited Bill already and knows where they're keeping him.

I'm ready as hell, Abi, let's go kidnap the boy.

So we walk through the hospital doors and she guides the way.

Abilena

Guess in the end we're the thieves. Feel like I'm outside my body watching us walk the hallways of the hospital, nobody paying any mind to the old man and his daughter. Him five feet and eight inches tall with yellow-white hair flatlocked to a leather skull and blue eyes recoiling into the handsomely carved bone. A body like wet rope sealed to itself, with the feet of an ape and the kneecaps of an awkward child. Her almost as tall, with the graceful flesh of a body born naked, flesh to which cloth is a hindrance. She has a generous, proportionate face with curious eyes. The girl's also hunched slightly, as if hung from some sapless higher branch. Both of them are spotted with myriad brown moles, familiar and grotesque like the smell of a bygone incestuous memory. They tread lightly in mud-spattered boots, him keeping watch, her soundlessly turning the door handle. Until we disappear into Bill's room.

William

Something ugly's stewing for the old man. I can see it in the details of his face. The faint trembling of his eyelid. The sweat beading on his upper lip. The horrible smell of his breath. He's real close to my face, looking at me.

Bill. Can you hear me in there?

(Yes. Fuck off, you worthless piece of garbage.)

We're here.

(She visits often. Why are you here?)

Then dad turns to Abi and speaks to her.

What do these machines do? Aren't we gonna kill him by unplugging them?

(Wait a second, you fucking moron, don't you make any decisions. Don't you do anything at all. Don't fucking touch me. Get the fuck out of this room and don't come back. Go kill yourself like you should have years ago.)

I doubt it. I think they're just monitoring him.

What about this thing going into his belly?

It's a feeding tube. We're gonna have to be careful with it.

(Wait, wait.)

And when he's with us, we gotta feed him.

How do we do that?

We'll have to bring mash. Liquid things. Fish oil. I saw his nurse feed him a couple of times.

Then dad's rough finger draws a circle around the hole in my stomach and he holds the flesh quite delicately and pulls the tube out. (The hands you used to beat me with, you fucking coward. If the world could only see how pathetic you are, threatened by a child, competing with a little boy. If they could only see what I've seen.) It hurts less than I expected.

So we're gonna carry him with that? What is it?

An old parachute bag I fixed up. You'll have to help me strap him in.

(No.)

I'll do the carrying.

(Don't touch me.)

Ok. Let's not hurt him.

We won't. Don't worry Bibi. Grab the red bottle. And

the tape. Do you see any bandages?

Yes.

Grab those. We need to disinfect the hole and patch it up.

(Don't touch me you fucking asshole. Where's Isabel? Where the fuck are you when I need you, Isabel?)

Any extra bandages?

Yes.

Keep them. Tape too. We'll need both. And take the mercurochrome.

After they're finished with the hole in my stomach, they dress me in a jogging suit and strap me to dad's back, facing away from him. It's like riding backwards on a rollercoaster.

Is he ok?

He looks fine.

Make sure the straps aren't crushing his balls. No man deserves that.

(Now I'm a man?)

They're fine dad.

Good. Now grab the tarp, Abi, we need to cover him. If they see him, we're fucked.

(Stop. The fucking yellow tarp's suffocating me. Abi don't do this. Stop him.) But actually I'm breathing fine beneath it. They sound quieter now, carrying me through the hospital. The old man's straining his back. Good, the fucker. (You two idiots are out of your fucking minds.)

Abi, they're gonna notice.

No dad, they aren't. You're just a backpacker.

It's too big to be a backpack, Bibi.

Just walk and shut up.

Then I hear the voice of a male nurse. (We're fucked.)

Señor. Señor.

Yes?

You can't bring your backpack in here.

Oh. I'm sorry.

Leave it at the entrance. We have a storage room for luggage.

Thank you.

It's just down the hall. Right there.

Thanks but I've changed my mind. I think I'll come back without it.

Suit yourself. *Hasta luego señor.*

Jesus, that was close.

The light of day is shining through the yellow tarp and the wind's blowing the plastic against my face.

You can see his feet poking out!

Jesus christ, Bibi. What an idiot. Let's get Bill to the car before that guy figures out what happened.

(Leave me here. Just leave me here. Don't push me in there. Don't. I fucking hate this car. It smells like dad.) They lay me down on the warm back seat and I can see the sky through the blackened glass of the rear window. Dad starts the car and the vibrations fill my lungs and legs and every part except the feet and fingers, which I can't feel anyway. (She'll never touch my asshole again. I hope they crash the car and we all die.)

Daniel

I share the double bed with Bibi and we lay Bill on the folding army cot so he doesn't have to sleep alone. Can't hear anything except my breathing, on account of I'm going nuts, sweating and flopping around in the sheets. Thinking about how much I hate this house. I'd burn it to the ground if I could, for the amount of times I've been dead drunk on that couch upstairs. For Sarah's television room. For the wood of Bill's door. For everything I've failed to be. But instead we'll be fugitives. My daughter, my son, and anything left of what I am. Bill's eyes are open, the moonlight shining in them like those fish bellies filling the lake. Abi seems to be asleep til her words float through the dark.

Dad.

Yes, Bibi?

Why do we have to leave tomorrow morning?

They'll be looking for us.

Who?

The house people. The bank people. The lake people. They're all the same.

But isn't this our house?

Never. I don't own a damn thing. And you should see

the lake. Nobody's gonna be fishing there ever again.

What about the fishermen?

I don't know Bibi. Never been much good at taking care of people.

You know I have a bit of money set aside from the paintings. Nothing that'll pay the debts, but if it can help.

Good, it'll buy us a proper tent. We need gear and supplies.

And then what?

We head into the mountains.

And once they find us?

We keep going. I'm done with Caracas. This place is gonna sink right into the ground. Take us all with it. We can go to Uruguay. The politicos out there used to be *tupamaros*. I hear they keep the *gringos* in check.

Dad, you're a *gringo*.

I hear there's some nice beaches in Uruguay. *Punta del Diablo*.

Can we take Bill with us?

Always.

Should we close his eyes so he can sleep?

Don't know. Don't think it'll make much of a difference. Let him watch the moon while he still can.

Abilena

I lay my head on dad's chest. He makes a crown from his index and thumb and binds me to his beating heart. Cause a brute's blood runs warmer than most.

I hope Mom's alright.

I think so, Bibi. She never had much use for me.

You gonna stop drinking?

I'm gonna try.

It'd be nice if you did.

I know.

Then I lie on my half of the bed and my eyes begin to close. The rain falls, cooling the air. It blows in long drafts, over the parts that lie awake. Dad smells of stale liquor.

Cause in my first dream the red heron's done cleaning and the river's packed with blood and guts. Nothing but the lone bird standing at the center of the stench. No other life. A dreadful stillness under the sun. Then it turns its black eye towards me and takes off in my direction.

William

The *blancanieves* looks like crystal sulfur and we're experimenting in biology class. When I make a line it's hard to chop cause it's too moist. My nose goes numb immediately and the taste in the back of my throat is numb too. Chemical. The roots of my teeth are numb and the palate of my mouth feels scraped and numb

Livingston is looking over and he can see what we're doing, Nesto, what are we gonna

They know I've been cutting it with caffeine pills and selling it to the locals, even though I asked them to shut the fuck up about it. *Rojo Flaco* isn't hard to find

His pockets are leaking crystal sulfur

Report to the principal's office, you little dunce. I'm sick of you screwing around in my classroom!

(He really was sick of my screwing around, and to be honest he was a good teacher and I still remember some of his lessons. Something about sublimation and compound elements.) Is that *cocaina*? Report to the principal's

Holy shit they're at my door and they're gonna cut my balls off and feed them to me. I'm transferring the coke from bag to bag, but there's a hole in the bottom of the plastic and there's yellow crystals everywhere on the fucking rug, it's gonna be impossible to hide all this shit

I'm on my knees sniffing the carpet and my whole face is numb now, but they're breaking into the apartment wearing black balaclavas

Tupamaros? No, probably the syndicates

One of them puts a chain around my neck and I'm a naked dog getting sodomized by a rifle

Another is about to piss on my face but his prick opens up and starts screaming

Abi's screaming in her sleep and dad's snoring right through it, the useless motherfucker. The drunk piece of shit that he is. I'm not moving, eyes wide open, bathing in sweat from that fucking dream. If Abi doesn't close my eyes, they're gonna dry up and I'll go blind in a few days. I guess it's better than dreaming.

Blancanieves y los siete enanos

Daniel

The criminal slum dwellers are eating up the *ávila's* roots, rotting its foothills with red brick, bad cement and rusty sheet metal. They're spilling down the mountainside and spreading like locusts over the flatlands. Most of em'll kill for a couple *bolos*.

I seen a naked kid stab a teenager for his shoes once. He was just a little scruffy-faced bastard too, cold as a snake. Kept going til the other kid stopped moving. I remember watching him quietly from my car, waiting for Maria Rita to come out of her place. Kid took the sneakers right off the other kid's feet and wore them like he was leaving a store. They were too big for him and he looked crazy, the naked with blood splashed on his face and hands, scruffy black hair and a shiny belly. It's the nature of what we're dealing with here. The world's going to shit. Me included. I watched him do it and just kept reading the paper. Thought about it later, how maybe that's not normal, to just shrug it off so easily. Maybe something's in the water. Something bad. Maybe the *gringos* want us fighting and killing each other.

But it's too early for crime as I drive through the slums. Night's finished but the sun hasn't risen, just a pale white mist over everything. Abilena's sleeping and Billy's doing his usual bug-eyed thing. Even the roosters stay quiet on account of nobody's proud at this hour. You're either working or praying or feeling awful about the whole business, and rightfully so. Light ain't even bright, just plain as hell. Nothing worse'n seeing exactly what you've done, no more, no less. It's unbearable.

So we drive down the dusty old street, swerving to avoid the goddamn potholes. They'll bust the axle right off this old bitch. She's no jeep. Any other driver and she'd be dead by now, but not me, I'll drive her right through the shackland and into the green. With Bibi sleeping on the dark red leather, head propped against her brand new sleeping bag. Waterproof. Keep her safe at night. Thank god she had some money cause I woulda had to rob the place. No way we could do this without supplies. But Bibi's never been tight with her money. She knows what it's for. Can't take it with you. Might as well have a good time while you can. Not that this is any party. Even Bill's wearing a serious look today. His eyes a little paler than I remember them. Light green. Turquoise. Sorta rough like a turtle's skin. Looking serious, as if he knows what we're up to and doesn't approve. I can feel the delirium starting too. The shaking and edges going threadbare. Not long now before I start to feel real horrible. But I won't bring a goddamn bottle of whiskey up there with me, cause I know this is my last chance. If I fuck this up, I'll lose these two. Sleeping Bibi and staring Bill. What a fucking family. Floating through the mist of sleeping shacks with the mountain rising dark and wet with life. Floating into the grey place where gods used to live.

Abilena

Countless tiny hands are squirming against the car window when I wake up. Above them the mouth of a donkey, filled with rotten teeth, pressing his clumsy tongue to the glass.

Good morning, *burro*.

He clacks his teeth in response and the children jostle around the car to look at the redheaded boy with his unblinking eyes and the blonde girl shaken by dreamsweats. Dad's nowhere to be found. The children scatter when I smile at them, only to regroup as I look away. There's a sticky film of white on Bill's eyes and I can tell he's going blind. I struggle to close his eyes cause the lids are caught on his dessicated eyeballs. Then the children watch me kiss him on the forehead. He looks dead now. Not just dead like he already is, but dead without a heartbeat. Even though it isn't cold, I pull a blanket over his knees and tuck it around his thighs.

Shit, we forgot the diapers. Bill's gonna need to do his business and they had diapers for him at the hospital. Where the hell's dad? And glancing around I can see we're in a village at the base of the mountain. Chicken coops of pulled wire, rusted walls of green blue corrugate, wood aged by the rains and hammered by the sun. Wild shrubbery lining the floodcarved dregs of ancient dirt paths. Fences overhung by foliage, trunks tethered and straining at their barbs. And by some miracle the black wires, drug along the valley and strung to woodstripped poles to feed the televisions.

I roll down the window and the kids stand back.

Dónde estamos?

But none of them answer. They keep whispering to each other.

Rubia. Rubia.

Like they've never seen blonde hair before.

Where is this?

One of the little ones stands forward to answer me.

Los Cujicitos.

Sweet kid with big brown eyes and a scar stretching from his flat nose all the way to his upper-lip.

Y mi padre? Where's he?

The man from the car, *señorita?*

Yes, where did he go?

The kid points a dirty finger down a crud path. It's a cul-de-sac leading to a whitewashed shack framed by dead weeds. I step out of the car and this time the kids stand their ground. They've heard me speak and they're not scared of me anymore. I want to lock the car but can't find the key. Must've kept it on him.

Hey, kid.

Sí?

Will you keep an eye on my brother for me?

Sí, por supuesto.

What's your name?

Luis Miguel.

Ok little guy. You're in charge.

What do I get in exchange?

What do you want? I don't have much to give.

Let me touch your hair.

I can do that. But only after you keep my brother safe and nobody takes anything from the car.

He stiffens and puffs his chest.

Por supuesto, señorita.

Good. I'll be back.

And I can hear them whispering as I walk away.

She dresses like a boy.

What's wrong with him? Is he dead?

But she's pretty.

Shut up. I saw her first.

He's breathing.

You're too young, idiot.

I'll make you shut up.

Calm down you two, she'll be gone and you'll still be brothers. Always the same when a girl comes around.

Who asked you?

Til I reach the shack. Already from outside I can tell what it is. Reeks to high heaven of cheap liquor and rancid sweat.

Daniel! You come out here this minute!

Bibi!

His voice jovial from inside the place.

Don't you Bibi me. I never shoulda married you to

begin with!

Silence in the shack. So I step through the doorway. Two men sit on milk crates in the semi-darkness with my father. Bottles line the wall, held up by a few rotten boards.

Bibi! This is Roberto and Chico.

Their blood-rimmed eyes barely register my presence.

Hijo de puta. I married a drunkard. You get your ass out of this shithole and take responsibility for your family.

Bueno, hombres. I think it's time to say goodbye. You know how it is with women. I'm sure you both have wives of your own.

Silence. I'm not certain they're even breathing. Dad jaunts through the doorway, spry as a young man.

You idiot.

Just one last, Bibi. After this there's not much ahead.

I'm sure you'll find some.

He gets serious suddenly.

I won't. I'm gonna have to face this thing once and for all.

So I don't say anything til we get to the car. He shoves

the kids aside and steps into the driver's seat. Before we leave I crouch to let Luis Miguel touch my hair. He rolls the locks between his thumb and forefinger slowly, pulling the curls straight just to watch them bounce back.

You're pretty too, kid. Don't be a show-off.

He looks at me a little hurt. I stand up and ruffle his hair.

See you when I see you.

In the rear-view mirror I can already see the other children piling onto him.

Dad, we have to stop for diapers.

Shit. That's right. I think there's a store near the control point.

Sure?

Yes.

Hope those *Inparques* fuckers don't give us a hard time.

They're stooges. Let me handle it.

Why're Bill's eyes closed?

He's resting.

Good. Hope he'll be able to walk soon.

Asshole.

Sorry, wife. Can't believe how you handled those two fellas. They went mute. Must've thought. That poor drunk. His wife's a real handful.

Just drive straight and don't kill us on the way.

Yes, wife.

And don't call me that.

He smiles at me.

Abilena, you're a real fucking woman, I can't believe it sometimes.

Dad.

Yes?

Shut the fuck up.

William

People think darkness is empty but I know it's teeming with words and sounds. They start small and convulse to life, rippling across the stillness only to vanish again like objects cast into a bottomless lake. The blind already know this: sound is simple and transparent, but words are a terrible cancer.

The words of those we love only die when we do.

(They are crippled phantoms limping in endless concentric circles.)

The words of my father: You're pathetic, Bill. You're too sensitive. Too complicated. Too smart for your own good. (Choking me against the wall.) Be a man. Take responsibility. Watch your mouth. You watch that mouth of yours. (Hovering behind me as I sit on the sofa reading.) I'm gonna count to three, then things aren't gonna go well. Do you hear me? Do you fucking hear me? (Across the dinner table as mom weeps in the bathroom.) You're doing this to your mother, Bill. You're killing her. (Waving me off.) Oh, you know your mother. Don't listen to her. She's hysterical. (Slapping me.) Don't talk back to your mother, you little shit. I know the truth about you, Billy boy (slurring on his knees next to my bed), you're trying to fuck me. But I'm not gonna let you. You get that into your head. (Tapping my skull with his fingers and biting his lip.) You get that into your little fucking head.

The words of my mother: (Angry.) That's no way for a son to speak to his mother. I'm going to wash your mouth out with soap. (Sad.) You used to be such a lovely child. So well-behaved. Now you've become a real pain. I don't know if I can trust you anymore. (Threatening quietly.) Do you know what happens to liars, William? (Pulling her hair back violently, strands floating in the air behind her as they catch on the silk curtains.) Why is your father doing this to me? I don't know if I love him anymore, William. (Shoving the back of my head with her sharp nails.) Smell your father. Smell him.

The words of Abilena: (Simple and looking at me.) I don't want to live in your world, Bill.

They prop me up in the back seat and feed me. Abilena sounds frustrated.

Open your mouth, Bill.

(I can't, you fucking idiot.)

Come on, Billy.

(Open it for me, *pequeña*.)

And she does. First I feel the cold metal of the spoon, then the sharp taste of applesauce.

Swallow, Bill.

(Fuck you.)

But somehow I do. A reflex of the nervous system.

He's eating it all up.

Don't make him too fat, Bibi. I gotta carry him.

After the applesauce there's black beans, mashed into a flavorless puree. Then fish oil, which stays caught in my throat and causes me to swallow repeatedly.

(Stop.)

I don't think he likes the fish oil much.

But he needs it, Bibi. The boy can't survive on apples and beans. Give him some water.

His lips seem dry.

She applies chapstick to my lips and pulls down my jogging pants.

(Please don't look at my tiny prick lying dead in my pants like a curled up little worm.)

The diaper feels safe and comfortable and I don't piss immediately. Better wait til the next changing instead of sitting in it. Even the hole from the feeding tube doesn't hurt much, just a hollow ache below my heart. Then I listen to the motor heaving and grinding, and dad tapping the steering wheel

(stop it stop it you motherfucker you dumb motherfucker I wish I could slit your throat with a razor blade and watch you bleed out in the mud or slam your head in the car door until it turned into a bloody pancake)

and Abi wetting her lips every seven to ten breaths.

(Stop. For fuck's sake.)

It's a relief to hear dad speak again when he finally does.

Ok, Bibi. The guardhouse is coming up. Let me do the talking.

You're drunk.

I'm not the only one, Bibi. Everybody's drunk in this fucking country. Been drunk since eighty-three.

Just concentrate on getting us into the park.

Fucking christ, Bibi, look at Billy back there.

(What is it this time?)

Do something about him. Push him over and pull up the blanket or something.

You want me to cover him?

No. Too suspicious. Leave his head poking out so they

think he's sleeping.

You coulda told me earlier, dad.

Shut up, shut up.

Hola señor. Señorita.

Hello. How're you guys doing?

(Nice small-talk you fucking idiot.)

Señor, are you transporting any wildlife into the park?

Course not.

Here to hunt?

Nope.

Any weapons in the car? Knives? Guns?

None.

Gardening tools?

Course not.

What's the purpose of your visit?

Bringing my kids here to the top.

Is this your wife?

Daughter.

And that's your son?

Sure is.

He asleep?

Yes sir.

What's wrong with him?

He's retarded, *señores*. Born simple.

Then there's a bit of silence and some shuffling paper. Dad breathing heavily. He reeks of liquor but apparently they don't care.

Bueno señor, you can go.

Thanks *hombres*.

And the motor grinds on.

Good job, Bibi. You can sit Bill upright again.

(Thanks, you piece of shit.)

What're we gonna do now that we're in?

We'll drive as far as we can. Then we'll ditch the old banger and make our way on foot. You're gonna have to help me with the gear.

I can do that.

You're a strong girl, Bibi, I knew it the day you were born. I'm sorry we couldn't bring your painting stuff.

It doesn't matter.

Still, you're a great painter.

(I'm nothing to nobody and I don't deserve anything.)

I do like painting, but in the end the *ávila*'s still better than any painting of it. And Bill's here and you're here, even though you're drunk as a skunk and always will be.

(No shit.)

Don't worry. I'll pay for it. I'll pay for it heavy.

(Yes, you fucking will. Just wait.)

Are you gonna be able to carry Bill?

Mostly.

Cause I can't carry Bill, not for long anyway.

We'll figure it out.

(We're all gonna die up there.)

Then they sit in silence for a long time. I can smell liquor and applesauce and slow farting. It feels like heaven on the way out. I miss Isabel, cause it won't be the same with Abi, even if she does it right, cause she's my sister and I can't feel good when she cleans my asshole. (Never stopped you in the past, did it now, with those thoughts about, no no no, what was the dream again, pissing inside her, stop, no, think of something else)

(Nesto, I guess you got to have everything. Fuck my sister and marry another *puta* from a rich family, leaving me in the gutter, you fucking son of a bitch. Stop)

The old man's got no idea. I remember the comedown at the hospital like it was yesterday. After they did the whole intervention and pumped me full of someone else's blood. I lay there all doped up and they stitched my arms. Could barely feel anything til the heroin started leaving my system and the ground gave out. I remember the ache in every bit of my body, thick and brutal. Every vein, every artery, every cell of it, from the tips of my fingers to the end of my nose. My toenails ached. All I needed was a shot but the doctors didn't know I was a junkie then, just figured I was an attempted suicide. They were running around trying to figure out why my vitals were so fucked up. Then the heat came, like no other heat in the world. I was boiling alive, my sliced-up arms like flames burning hot through the flimsy stitches. Then the cold, sweeping through like a black wind. That's when they started realizing what I was.

He's convulsing. He may be having a seizure. Diazepam. One milligram. And the needle in my arm. Again. And the needle again. The slight relief painting my nerves, gluing my body to the unbearable pain. Kill me. Kill me. Or inject me again. Just shoot my body with anything. You cocksucking automatons. Find Abi or I'll die. I'll kill every single one of you, smash your skulls with a chair. Please kill me. Just a little. My stomach's gonna burst into my lungs. My lungs are gonna burst into my neck and shatter my spine into my brain. My brain's gonna boil out of my skull and shoot through the top of my head. My skin's sucking my blood. My bones are gonna shatter and spread their shards through the muscles. Guts gonna shrivel and the gas gonna fill them til they burst into flames like ice-cold fireballs shrinking into my skull to crack my mouth gumless. Until sleep came and I could hear the machines beeping and realized in horror that I might survive.

Once in a while a nurse came in to take my temperature and check my blood pressure. I could hear my heart's pathetic little beeping. Then I started shitting a steady stream of burning diarrhea and vomiting til they turned me on my side cause they thought I might choke on it like Hendrix. Tears were running down my face, hot fat tears til the tip of my nose. The vomit ran out, but my stomach kept racking into a coil and my lungs started seizing til I thought I was gonna suffocate. They shot me up with more diazepam and pulled an oxygen mask over my face. I immediately puked and almost drowned in the vomit pressed to my nose and mouth.

After a few more hours of this, everything finally started to settle down. For a few days it just felt like a bad flu. Isabel was by my side the entire time. She would speak to me softly, just like mom did when I had migraines as a kid.

Oh, Willy. You seem better today. So much better. I've seen dopesickness before, but nothing like this.

And she smoothed my hair with her hand.

Daniel

The car dies choked in the mist. Old banger's got nothing left in her. Always drank gas like I did whiskey. Well it looks like we're up shit's creek now, you old whore. But I don't wake Bibi yet. Instead I bite the worn leather of the steering wheel and let my hand run the dashboard, feeling my blood turn hot and cold. End of the line. Time to go. But Bibi's face looks so peaceful and wise as she sleeps. She must be thirty now, and I'm an old man. No time for this. Why? There's lots of time. Not if the bends are coming. You better be somewhere safe by then. None of it matters. Shut up. Stop talking to yourself. You're gonna make yourself crazier than you already are. Take care of business. You wake her up.

Bibi. Bibi.

I shake her shoulders gently until her eyes jolt open and her skinny hand shoots out, gripping my wrist with ungodly strength.

No! Oh dad. It's you. Will you keep it away? Will you keep it away.

Then she's asleep again, hand slack, face pressed to my chest.

Keep what away?

But she just grumbles and makes mouth noises.

Bibi.

Yes.

Are you awake?

Okay.

But she doesn't move at all.

Are you awake?

Yes, okay.

And she sits up with her eyelids half-open.

Can you wake Bill up?

She looks at me funny. Looks at Bill.

You mean open his eyes?

Right. Maybe we should wait. Well. We're here, Abi.

Where?

She looks around, disoriented, a stupid kid again.

Far as we're gonna get with this car, Bibi.

How come?

She's dead. Out of gas.

Okay.

So let's get Bill strapped to me and we'll start walking.

Okay.

So I open the door and walk around the car. Pop the trunk and look inside. Tall backpack for Bibi with food and diapers and clothes. Small backpack for me with cooking equipment, canned goods, the gun, a hunting knife, a swiss army knife. Rope. Matches. Mosquito juice. The compass. A steel canteen. Pictures hidden at the bottom. And the old parachute.

Abi helps me pull Bill out of the car and holds him standing while I get his legs into the straps. Once he's fastened I crouch down and push my arms through. Tighten it properly.

He's lighter by the day. Billy bones.

Don't call him that.

I'm ready for the backpack.

Abi straps it to my chest. Then she hoists the big backpack onto her shoulders and fastens the clasps around her waist and above her breasts. She looks at me sorta desperate like there's nothing we can do and we're gonna die up here. She's probably right. It's my fault.

You alright, dad?

Fine, Bibi. Got everything. Wait. Shit. I left my smokes on the dashboard. Can you grab them for me?

Okay.

I light one and push the pack into my pocket.

Thanks.

Not too heavy?

It's okay.

Let's go then.

Where to?

Up through here.

And our first day in the mountains begins.

Abilena

Ahead of us of us lies a rock-strewn path disappearing into the mistlands. Not even a path really, just a carpet of dead leaves and woodchips pushing through the phalanxes of twisted trees. Like a monstrous hand descended from the sky to bend the saplings young cause it couldn't stand the sight of a trunk grown straight.

Beautiful, the way the pale green lichen flares on the knotted bark. I can even hear the fiery gnar of howler monkeys in the distance. There's a deep moist silence between their shrieks. It feels like we're underwater almost.

We walk for hours through ferns and brambles, sparse canopy overhead, til the mist thins to smokey dregs. And Dad looks like he's really starting to lose it.

Daniel

We gonna run into anybody, dad?

I doubt it. This ain't a tourist area. We're way off the beaten path. Hopefully no rangers either. They might not appreciate our little passenger.

Why?

Who knows. People get scared.

What about poachers?

What about them?

Do they exist?

Yes, they exist, Bibi. Can we stop it with the questions for a bit? I need to smoke a cigarette and walk a bit.

Fine.

So my feet press into the dirt, wet in parts, as we walk uphill through the fog. I light another cigarette. My legs feel strong. Bibi leading the way. Sickness bubbling its way. Patches of black maggots squirming in the moss. Then just moss. And Bill mute, limp, burning white.

I see the outline of trees with red fruit hanging in the branches. Long red fruit. Not fruit. Birds. Herons. No, there ain't a heron as red as that. Must be another bird. An ibis maybe. Not just one. Lots. A dozen at least. Hanging from their feet in the branches of the trees. Strung up with rope. Riddled with bullets. Used as shooting practice. What monster did I? Some of them are bleeding fresh. Others are rotting. Long pink beaks curved and dripping. Small black eyes accusing me. They know what I've done.

Bibi.

What?

Do you see that?

What?

The birds.

What birds?

In the trees, there.

I can't see anything.

The birds.

Are you ok, dad?

I'm fine, Bibi. Let's keep going.

Trees thicker now. More of them. Til we reach a small

clearing with the grey hump of a giant boulder in the middle. I sit Bill against its flank like a puppet when the show's over. Guess Bibi opened his eyes at some point, cause he's staring again. Green eyes sorta milky. So I go digging in Bibi's bag for some food. I have to steady my shaking hand to open the valve and fuel the flame. My heart's pounding hard and fast like I might die any minute. I can handle it. Pour some rice into the water. Stare at the pot. Steam licking my face. Too hot. Then too cold. The angry eyes of a hundred spiders. Just bubbles in a pot. The water's boiling. Bibi's eating some grapes. She's mashing them with her teeth, spitting them into her palm, and pushing them into Bill's mouth like a mama bird. Then she makes him drink water from the canteen. We cut open a can of beans with the hunting knife and pour them into the drained rice. Abi scrapes the goop into the metal bowl and crushes it with her fork, then pours the fish oil directly into it and tries feeding Bill. He refuses. Food sits limp between his lower lip and teeth. She's angry.

Come on you stubborn idiot. I know it's fishy but you gotta eat.

And he loosens slightly. Then he's swallowing again.

Bibi.

Yes?

Do you like him?

Who?

Bill.

Of course I do.

Well, he's your brother. But other than that.

Yes.

Why?

Cause he was a decent older brother til he got into drugs. Bill taught me how to draw. How to look at the object instead of the line. And took me crabbing. Taught me how to think hard about something. How to do something intensely. How to stop caring what other people think.

She feeds Bill patiently. I can hear the birds and monkeys talking and they're saying I've been a shitty father just like my old man. I stare at Bibi. Her face is glowing with a sweaty death. She'll carry on my suffering just like Billy did. She's gonna hurt and I can't do anything about it. The world is gonna destroy everything I care about, and I know how. Cause I'm the hired gun.

Bibi.

Yes.

Did I ever teach you anything? Anything good or

useful?

She stops feeding Bill for a moment and looks at me. She's gonna push the fork into my eye. She's gonna kill me.

Yes you did, dad.

What?

My love for

Abilena

Everything alive is beautiful and dangerous. So if you let things in, they might hurt you bad or even kill you, but if you keep them out you'll surely die. Cause like the shell of the cicada, your shape'll remain standing, but you'll be long gone. So only an idiot thinks there's a choice to be made. That's why I'm in the mountains with Bill and Dad. Cause they're the most beautiful and dangerous animals in the world. But they're like the red sickness too, spreading everywhere inside me with nothing to do about it. And Mom's out on a farm somewhere along the *Rio Tocuyo*, a place where there's no movies with Harrison Ford in them, where she's gonna find her own life, cause she was queen of the expats til the betamaxes fell, and now she's probably queen of the goats. I imagine her leaving footsteps in the dirty sand, washing clothes from the riverbanks and hanging them to dry on desiccated bushels, living in the wild where breasts don't matter, where she can untie her hair and bathe in the currents. That's how she lives in my daydreams.

Bill's done eating and I wipe his chin with some leaves. Our clothes are damp and he's trembling. The sun's doing a bad job. I slap my arm and my hand comes back bloody. A crushed mosquito twitching in the blood.

Where's the bug repellent?

In my bag, Bibi. I'll get it.

I'm gonna rub Bill down. He's already bit up. It's not fair really, cause he can't defend himself.

You ready to keep going?

You don't want any?

I'm fine. Nothing much to feed them here. My blood's probably just poison. If you see a swarm of mosquitoes flying in zigzags, you know why.

And dad smiles tensely. So I rub repellent on my arms and neck and face.

We got four hours til sunset. Let's keep going.

Alright.

So Dad pulls Bill into a standing position and props him against the rock. I slip my arms under his pits and pin him to the boulder. Face pressed to the moss like this, Bill looks like a stupid dog waiting for a door to be opened. I shiver. Once Bill's strapped to Dad's back, I attach the small backpack to his chest again. Then I swing the big one over my shoulders and fasten the straps. My hips are sore where the weight rests, but no matter.

It's time to abandon the clearing and march without thinking through the chaparral until the mist begins to fall away, revealing crooked trees and boulders rising through the forest floor like patches of mange on a dog's rump. Soon the canopy disintegrates and we find ourselves above the clouds.

Dad, turn around so Billy can see. Look.

The sun's dipping white, dragging its yellow rim through the orange sky. Caracas is barely visible, cloaked beneath a grey-white blanket of cumulus billowing unhurriedly across the valley. I can see distant ranges in layers of grey and mauve, their peaks orbited by rogue scudders.

We're here, Billy. You're out of the *barrio*.

Can I turn around yet, Bibi?

Don't you fucking dare, it's Billy's turn to see something beautiful.

I'm gonna put him down anyway, Bibi. We'll camp right here.

On the rock?

On that patch over there. The moss'll make it gentle and the rock'll keep us dry.

So I lay my backpack on the ground. Then I sit spread-eagle with my spine against the bag, facing the valley with Bill in my arms. Make sure his eyes are open so he can see the whole thing. The way things can be. If you just look.

William

In the distance I can see the world I killed myself for. I've lost feeling in my hands and feet but my heart still beats at the center, stubbornly driving blood through my torso. Since yesterday there's been a faint prickling atop my skull, like wet wood whistling in a bonfire. Smell is totally gone but I can hear better than ever. Even the slow drift of clouds in the valley makes a low-pitched squeaking, like a shoe being shined in slow motion. Abi kisses my cheek and holds me close. I see it, Abi. I can't do anything about your crying, but I can see the sun's descent into the valley of clouds. I know what the city looks like from your arms and I don't feel alone.

Daniel

The stakes won't drive past the moss, so I tie each corner of the tent to a good rock. The wind's pretty quiet anyhow, so we should be good for the night. My skin's crawling and my insides are moiling just to keep me alive. Bibi unravels the sleeping bags and pulls some crackers and cottage cheese from the backpack.

What are we gonna feed Bill?

I kept some rice and beans from earlier, gonna give him that.

Poor bastard. Nothing worse than fish oil.

Aren't you gonna have any food?

Not hungry.

Dad, you should eat something.

Not hungry, I'm going for a walk.

When are you coming back?

In a bit.

What's a bit?

Don't worry, Bibi.

But she's showing me her teeth. My daughter's gonna kill me in my sleep. Better get far away from the tent so I can shit without hallucinating. But it's impossible to outrun the boiling green forest.

Papa's gonna whip me good. Been out too long.

I'm the Papa now. I'm in charge. I'm gonna whip me good.

I'm gonna shit like a bear in the woods. She's gonna kill me.

Stop and concentrate for god's sake. The delirium tremens. You're seeing things. You're being paranoid. You're on a walk through the simple woods. To shit. That's all. Then you'll return to the goddamn tent and get some sleep. Concentrate now. So you don't shit your pants like a baby.

Baby gonna whip.

Trees falling one by one. Died crushed to death by a pile of fucking trees. With his pants down.

Nobody's out here. Trees too thin to hide men. Dangerous men standing sideways. Nobody's watching you shit. But I feel their eyes on my bare skin. Steady my shake on the trunk of an old man's leg. Shitting hot and cold.

I promise I'll be good. I promise I'll be good. Just get

me through.

It's an inside job. A fucking coup. They set up a tent where my arteries are, the shadowy fucks. I shit til I'm empty but the cramps won't stop, so I lie in the moss, away from the smell. Notice night crawling through the leaves to choke me out. Military men are leaning over me to operate my guts but they're using old fishbones and rusty gutting knives.

You said I'm a good fisherman, but I died so you could make money off the rotten *gringos*. Ain't it true, Danny? Ain't it true?

Javier, you fell into the fucking lake. I'm supposed to make you wear a lifejacket now?

You never even fished me out. I'm still down here. Til I got tired and lonely and started poisoning the water. Soon I'm gonna climb out of the lake and pay you a visit, *jefe*. Count on it.

Fuck off, Javier.

Hey boss, why didn't the other *gringos* tip you off? They all made millions buying dollars before black friday. Why'd they leave you out?

Because I'm a fucking nigger to them. A *morocho*. I'm working class scum like you.

No you're not, boss. You're lower. You're a man who

tried to be a profiteer and failed.

Shut up, Javier. Shut the fuck up.

I'm lying on the moss and I can feel the hunting knife sheathed in my back. You're out in the woods alone. Shitting. Why did you bring a knife? You're done shitting. Now you're lying on your back. Nobody's doing nothing. What are you scared of?

But I can hear the woods creaking. I can hear the bugs and the birds and the crawlers. The CIA ordered them folks dead. So many bodies. On account of I'm going crazy. You're nuts. Must be the moss or the dying. I'm dying. Either way I close my eyes and it's off to the fucking races, the chittering won't stop and the insects are crawling all over me. Even the birds are gonna chew my lips off.

Abilena

Change Bill's diaper and lay him in a sleeping bag. Smooth his purple eyelids and kiss his cheek.

Time to rest, Billy. Or should I call you Snow White. *Blancanieves.* Cause you're so beautiful and pale.

Then it hits me. Through the chirruping darkness, through the sound of moths beating their wings against the tent walls. How tired my body is. Feet sore, hips bruised, back aching. Feels good to lie down. Wanted to wait for dad, but can't help shutting my eyes. Leave the flashlight on. Dad'll find the tent. He wouldn't abandon us.

I can see stars through the darkness of my closed lids, but the moon's nowhere to be found.

Jorge

Think they carryin a corpse. Say hey zero, they're carryin a fuckin corpse. Pass me the binoculars. Wait a second. Cause I'm lookin at her. She ain't half ugly the little bitch. Dressed like a fuckin farmer, a *campesina*. Nothin you can't cut off. Lemme see. Shut up a second. The man looks old and tired. Nothin I can't handle. The equipment though. Everythin real shiny. Them's fuckin *Gringo* brands. Maybe some lost tourists. Probably cameras in there. Cash. Watches. Credit cards. Jewelry. Maybe jewelry. What's with the corpse though? Zero keeps openin his stupid gob. Fuck, Jorge. Gimme the fuckin binoculars. Here. Shove em up your ass. And I toss em at him. You sonuvabitch. Looks like they're settin up they camp. That's no corpse, he says. How d'you know, I says. Cause it's got eyes open. And she's sittin with it. Looks more like a fuckin retard. Gimme those back. Wait a second, you fuckin sonuvabitch. You'll get em soon enough, he says. Stupid cunt zero. Shoulda kept my mouth shut. Shoulda ditched him. Be here alone to rob these tourists. But I know he ain't got the stomach for crime, zero doesn't. I'm gonna rob em, zero. Shut up, Jorge. I'm gonna rob em, I says again to his face. Not with him around you ain't. He's just an old man. I'm gonna kill him first and then I'm gonna cut his eyes out and feed em to the girl. I'm gonna cut his prick off and fuck her with it. Zero keeps the binoculars up and turns to look at me. No you ain't. I told you what I'm gonna do, so now you can take it or leave it, I says. I ain't tryin to kill nobody, he says. You told me it wouldn't be like that. Well I lied, I tell him. You sonuvabitch Jorge, you sonuvabitch. You fucking twisted sonuvabitch. Looks at me real crooked. Then he puts down the binoculars, spits, and slings his bag. Fuck you, he says. Then he disappears into the trees. Zero ain't smart. What he don't know is that I ain't plannin to kill nobody but I ain't plannin to share neither. I wouldn't do nothin. God know that. I'm a good man in my heart. Mama know that. Sometimes I forget that, but then I remember it later, so I'm nothin bad. I pick up the binoculars and settle in til night comes round and their tent's up. Can't see him no more. Probably restin in the tent. She pops her head out and looks round like a mouse in the dark. All the bags are inside. Then she zips the door up. So I wait another hour and start creepin down the ridge, holdin trees as I go, gun stuffed down my jeans. I can be pretty quiet, specially at night.

Daniel

I can hear it circling, smell its filthy fur, its rotten teeth clacking, its wet tongue lapping, cause I've been crouching and waiting for the beast to show its face, and I'm ready for it. Got my hunting knife out, but I won't barely need it, cause I'll use my teeth, and every single leaf of the forest floor's listening with me. This is where it ends. I've been waiting all my life for this, Papa, sharpening my knife and whittling wood and slicing fish, cause I knew the day'd come it'd be me and you circling each other in a dark forest til one of us lies in a bloody pulp, and it ain't gonna be me, so I shift my knife from left to right, gotta hold it tight, and everything's wet to cover the smell, so I'm just part of the night, no lie, even painted myself with mud, rubbed leaves under my arms and all around my balls. Nobody's smelling my fear cause I got none.

William

Abi's snoring again. My eyes are closed, but I'm neither sleeping nor thinking about the fucked up world. No pain. No voices. Can't summon anything to cover up the peaceful feeling of being a big dumb baby because pequeña changed my diaper. So I'm listening to the sound in layers: insects, birds, nameless foraging, and rubber boots on the wet mud. Not dad's, either.

Jorge

Get extra quiet near the tent. Ground wet. They asleep. Lots of jungle noises to cover my creepin. Just get the stuff. Keep your gun out. Keep it steady. Scare em. Fill one of em backpacks with stuff. Tell em to stay in they tent til mornin or you kill em. Make sure you show your face real serious. Tell em I'll kill you. Tell em I'll fucking kill you. Tell em don't believe me? Tell em I'll shoot the gimp. That bitch though? No. None of that. Just cameras, cash. Jewelry. Then get the fuck out. They got the lamp on. Maybe she afraid to sleep in the dark. So what. Circle to the left and peel up the window flap. Gimp and her, both sleepin. Guy not here. Just make it quick. Do it now and make it quick. So I unzip the tent door and point my gun. Nobody movin. Guess the gimp must be dead. She sleepin, hair spread wild, golden, tanktop pushed to the side. See the puff of her nipple. Keep the gun steady. Take the stuff. Just take the stuff and get out. But I get on my knees, real close to the pink skin. There's a mole right above it too. Puffed with lamplight. Young. Can't be older than twenty five, the little bitch. The wet little bitch. And that's when she wake up.

Daniel

The beast came, but it came for them. Hear my little girl yelling through the trees and start tearing across the forest.

Abilena

After I scream, there's a moment of silence and the man's face is caught in the plastic lamplight. There's a hideous scar running from the tip of his chin to his clavicle and his eyes are bloodshot in different colors, one yellow, one brown. They're too far apart to be friendly. His yellow teeth are biting his lower lip. He's unshaven, with a military cut and a camo jacket. His nostrils are flaring like a bull's and the muzzle of his revolver is trembling slightly, leveled at my chest.

Wiliam

This motherfucker smells like raw meat and piss. If you touch her I'll. (What. I'll what?)

Daniel

Got the beast in my sights now, the greasy tufts of his man-eating backside. He's already half inside the tent.

Jorge

She kickin and fightin the little bitch. Got my cock out my pants. It beatin with blood. I stand back and point the gun at her. Shut the fuck up or I shoot you right through the guts. Then her eyes get real wide.

Abilena

Behind the moon-faced man, some animal emerging from the darkness.

William

After her muted struggle the man yells at her and she goes quiet and then we all hear it: a guttural scraping. I can't even identify the animal.

Daniel

I plunge the hunting knife into its backbone and pull its head by the hair, tearing the soft part of the throat with my sharp teeth, but the beast spins like lightning and strikes me hard below the belt.

Jorge

Cut and hurtin but the pain ain't come yet. Some sorta maniac tryin to chew my neck off so I turn and kick his balls. He falls back on the grass and I point my gun at his fuckin head.

Abilena

All of it seems like a slow dream as the man pivots nightward, the back of his camo jacket stock-still in the ebbing lume, nape framed in the pitch black. For a moment he doesn't seem to be moving at all. I see wider than ever from inside the tent. I see Bill's open eyes, the pirouetting flashlight, and every raised hair on my outstretched arm. My wrist is steady and my index finger pulls at the cold black metal of the gun's trigger.

William

My eyes open with the bang, like some great machinery clapping to a halt and ringing out in the stillness. I guess Abi kept dad's fourty-four Magnum within reach.

Daniel

Got me down on my ass and I know I'm gonna die. I'm sorry Bibi. Useless til the end. Then thunder strikes the clouds and the beast pukes red-white mist, falling towards me to claw me ragged. I'm a goner.

Jorge

Soy los árboles mama, soy los

William

Everything above the man's shoulders disappears completely. It's the last thing I see before the cotton closes in.

Daniel

My guts are sliced and I'm bleeding to death. The beast's on top of me and he's dying too, somehow. Guess I finally did a good thing for my kids.

Abilena

I'm knocked over by the shot and I stay down for a while.

Time passes or doesn't pass. My ears are ringing.

I rise slowly on my sore elbows. Bill's white face is blanketed in pink dew, even his eyeballs have flecks of blood on them. It's everywhere inside the tent. I grab the flashlight and spring through the zipper, standing frozen over the shapes. There's total silence in the faunal hiss. I feel paralyzed, can't even point the flashlight. Then my body moves. I catch the dead man's jacket in the beam. His neck's leading nowhere, spewing dark gore. Dad's caught beneath him, mouth open, his soundless scream bubbling over with unfamiliar blood. The bodies are side-lit by the fallen flashlight. Dad's fingers are digging the dirt in agony. I grab the man's jacket with both hands and tug his corpse aside, blood jetting in an arch as he flips over. Then I pick up the flashlight and point it at Dad again. He coughs and sputters a fountain of black.

Bibi.

Dad.

I'm dying, Bibi.

I rip his t-shirt down the middle and use it to mop the blood from his chest and neck, holding the flashlight between my head and shoulder.

It's not your blood, dad.

He looks past me into the distance.

I'm dying. *Madre de dios.* I'm finally dying.

I wipe his face with the t-shirt.

There was only one shot, dad, you're gonna be fine.

You gotta get me the photos, Bibi.

What photos?

At the bottom. In the backpack. The photos. Just one last thing before I go. I gotta be with her. I gotta see her.

What are you talking about?

The photos. The fucking photos.

So I stand up and head back to the tent, pulling everything out of the backpack til I find a green plastic bag wrapped around a yellow envelope. It says KODAK. I walk back out into the stars.

I can't feel my arms, Bibi.

Yes you can. Do you want these or not?

His eyes seem to focus for an instant before he reaches

for the envelope. Then I watch him tremble as he pulls the pictures out.

William

I'm blind Bill.

Daniel

Gotta kiss Maria Rita's cunt before I go.

Abilena

Eventually the trembling lessens and Dad falls asleep clutching the dirty photos to his chest. The horizon shifts purple as I keep silent watch over him. After a few hours I slice up the rest of his clothes and run my hand along his knotted muscles to make sure I didn't miss anything. Nothing but bruises and age. Then I head back into the tent, close Billy's eyes, and

William

After she lowers my lids I start to see things clearly: her skinny legs and the moon. She chases the white crabs. *Pequeña.* I see her burying the bird beneath the avocado tree. The soiled hands and solemn face of a child in sacrament. I see my sister writhing on the filthy sofa, losing her baby. One by one by one, it's all gonna ease itself. Oh yes it will.

Daniel

I'm alive somehow. Get to my feet and stare at the rising sun of another morning. Dew covers the moss. At my feet lies the headless corpse of another soldier. My blood-caked clothes are cut to strips. Stained photos fall through my fingers as I rise. I must've. What did I do? Stumble to the stream and strip naked to lie in the cold current and feel life return. Whatever I did or didn't do. Whoever I am. God please let it pass in these waters.

Abilena

Dad shakes me into the day. We sacrifice two t-shirts to wipe down the essentials. Then we wrap the corpse in the tent and use fallen branches to build a pyre. The wood's still damp so it takes an hour to catch, then we search the surroundings and find three teeth still attached to a jawbone. No head. No bullet. No more teeth. They must have disappeared. There's chunks of white and grey and red and purple everywhere. Already birds are hopping round with bloody beaks. Even a *tapaculo* with its green wings and fiery chest pecks at the gore in disappointment. A quiet pair of brown foxes wander the area, licking the open ground. They keep their pale eyes on us as we pack our belongings. Ants, beetles, mosquitoes, and the absurd daylight cremation of a nameless man with different-colored eyes. Most of his blood's already drained into the soil. The rest is hissing and popping in the daylit flames.

EPILOGUE

Abilena

Bill died before the rains. It was a day like another. Daniel rose early to garden. I slept past dawn and opened my eyes to the familiar walls of the hut, sun filtering through the square windows' makeshift netting. In my dream the flamingoes had returned. They thronged the laguna, filling the air with the saw-like stringe of their birdcalls. I observed in disgust as they unwound their pink necks and lunged the muddy water for shrimp. Finally I turned away from the laguna and looked out over the ocean. In the sunset I beheld the flock of herons, scarlet daubs forming a shrinking V above the horizon. So I knew Bill's heart had settled for good. I didn't touch the corpse, but instead started making preparations for its burial.

Daniel

Dig it four foot deep, eight foot long, and three foot wide. My son's grave.

Abilena

The withered corpse lies bloodless among the easter orchids, skin graced by fading constellations of pigment. The sweet mingle of arrested bloom and necrotic flesh. Last rites in the form of a kiss.

Daniel

Swinging the shovel in wide circles, I avoid covering his face until it becomes impossible. Then my son disappears beneath the loose soil.

Abilena

Daniel wipes his brow with the frayed hem of his t-shirt, blue eyes glowing in the anemic daylight. He spits against the hillside and looks at his work.

That'll probably do. Just hoping there's no rain for a spell so the dirt can settle.

He drinks from the canteen and wipes his mouth with the back of his hand.

I'm leaving, Daniel.

I know, Bibi.

And he holds my gaze for a moment before I turn away.

ABOUT THE AUTHOR

Julian Feeld lives in Paris. He grew up in Uruguay, Switzerland, France, the USA, Venezuela, Brazil, and Canada. Even the Red Heron is his debut novel.

IF YOU ENJOYED THE NOVEL

(This in particular would be of great help!)
Please review it on goodreads.com and amazon.com

FOR NEWS ON FURTHER WORK

Twitter: @julianfeeld
Website: julianfeeld.com

ACKNOWLEDGMENTS

I am in debt to the following people: Kathleen Craig, for reading every day until the work was finished; Louisa Pillot, for her relentless encouragement; Alicia Heimerson, for allowing me to read out loud as she fell asleep (and enjoying it); and Genevieve Gagne-Hawes, for her work as an editor. Without the kind words of these four people, I would have ceased writing long ago. I would also like to thank all the crowd-funding campaign contributors, especially Audrey & Gerard Peverelli, Susan & Robert Edmondson, and Alain Galley. Finally, I would like to thank all the readers and writers, alive or dead, without whom I would not exist, much less write or experience joy. I bow to you all.

CPSIA information can be obtained at www.ICGtesting.com
Printed in the USA
LVOW05s1104020514

384204LV00003B/81/P

9 781495 414695